# TURN
# BACK
# TIME

MATTHEW RHOADS

ISBN 978-1-63874-353-8 (paperback)
ISBN 978-1-63874-354-5 (digital)

Christian Faith Publishing, Inc.
832 Park Avenue
Meadville, PA 16335
www.christianfaithpublishing.com

Printed in the United States of America

If you can look into the seeds of time and say which grain will grow and which will not, speak then to me.

—*Macbeth*, act 1, scene 3

For Heather

# Acknowledgments

I HAVE MANY TO THANK for the writing and completion of this novel. My parents were kind enough to look at every draft I completed and write numerous suggestions for corrections and additions that I could make. My wife and daughter told me several ways that the story might be improved. I used several books on Galveston history for researching the time and place in which the novel is set. Some examples would be *Galveston: A History of the Island* by Gary Cartwright, *Isaac's Storm* by Erik Larson, and *Through a Night of Horrors* by Cary Edward Greene and Shelly Henley Kelly. One could fill several shelves with all that has been written about the great island and city of Texas. I encourage the reader to find out for themselves. Special thanks to all the people at Christian Faith Publishing for their professionalism. Last but not least, I thank God with whom all things are possible.

**1**

SOMETIMES I WONDER IF I would have been better off not signing up for the time-travel experiment. Then again, I can't deny all the fun I've had in spite of the risks and complications. I've been through adventures and dangers most people will only experience vicariously through movies, television, or possibly a video game. Yet it's all been real for me. It's been that way ever since I became involved in the quantum molecular temporal displacement project, often called the QMTDP for short. It began with a call from an old college prof that I hadn't seen in a decade.

I was in my office at Galveston College entering final grades for my psychology classes when I got the call. It was the end of April, and the semester was nearly over. I was looking forward to a good summer break and some relaxation time. It was still spring, but it was the kind of spring that a state in the deep south is known for, so it was warm enough that you didn't need a coat. I knew it wouldn't be long before the freeways would fill with people driving to Texas beaches and tourist traps. State troopers would be on the prowl to catch speeding teenagers driving drunk and possibly doing other things even worse. After all, teenagers often view themselves as immortal. I would be taking it easy since I didn't have a full teaching load. I only taught one class in the summer. Other than that, I had plenty of time to do whatever I could think of that wouldn't get me in trouble. The phone ringing interrupted my thoughts of summer fun. I picked up and said, "Hello?"

"Hello, is this Dr. Mark Allen?"

"Yes, how may I help you?"

"That may take me a while to explain," the voice chuckled.

"Pardon me," I responded to the familiar voice. "Is this Professor Powell?"

"That's me, sonny!" He laughed as I recalled his affectionate nickname for me. "How are things your way?"

"Great! Loving my teaching job, which you predicted I'd be good at. How are things your way?"

He launched into a description of his situation, and we talked for several minutes about our lives since last parting. I'm not sure how long the conversation went on, but Powell eventually got to the point. "I'd love to chat longer, but I've got to tell you why I called," he said with a slightly serious sound in his voice.

"Go ahead," I encouraged him.

He sounded like he was clearing his throat. "Um, have you ever been interested in participating in an experiment?"

I paused for several moments that probably seemed as long to him as they did to me. "Maybe. Do I get paid?" I laughed.

"Oh, let me assure you, sonny," he replied pleasantly, "if you participate in this experiment, you probably won't care whether you get paid or not. I think it would be best if we met in person for me to disclose any more information. You interested in having a bite at a good restaurant with your favorite prof?" I caught his sarcasm when he referred to himself as my favorite, but he certainly did rate high in my esteem.

"Sure." I thought for a moment. "How about Fisherman's Wharf in the Strand? They've got good seafood."

"Right on," he replied. "I was thinking this evening at about six."

"Sure," I told him. We said our goodbyes and hung up. I wasn't sure what to expect, but I had a feeling of anticipation mixed with a touch of dread. All of sudden I recalled the time I starred in a production of *Macbeth*, a play by William Shakespeare. The title character is told by three witches that something dramatic is going to happen to him. I wondered if something just as dramatic was about to happen in my case.

Fisherman's Wharf is a restaurant located in the old waterfront section of Galveston, Texas, the city where I live and work. You can see ships and boats through the bay windows that line the back wall. The food is tasty and the atmosphere to my liking. It was packed when I got to the entrance, looking for Powell. I saw him easily enough. A man with thick gray hair, about six foot two, and rather lean. He was seated on a bench and wearing his usual teaching uniform: a nice pair of slacks with dress shoes and socks, along with a crisp blue dress shirt and blue sportscoat. He definitely stood out from the other people in the restaurant. Not only was he taller than many of them, but his dress clothes were quite a contrast from the casual outfits worn by the other patrons. He turned to look at me, and it was as if no time had passed between our last parting. He stood up and came toward me with his hand extended.

"There you are," he grinned. "My prize pupil! You've aged better than I have, but who hasn't?"

I laughed at his remark and shook his hand with enthusiasm. I may not have been his best student, but I was certainly one of his most admiring. I still had fond memories of taking his sociology class as I pursued a bachelor's degree with a major in psychology and a minor in history. He was the man who showed how a class could be taught in a way that was both informative and entertaining. He also showed a great love for all his students that made him popular. He knew how to demonstrate tough love to students who were falling behind in class so that they could decide whether or not they should stay or drop the course. Overall, Powell was simply a man who showed passion and devotion to everything he did. It was an attitude that seemed to magically rub off on the rest of us.

I was interrupted in my stroll down memory lane by Powell telling me he had already reserved a table which would be ready in a few minutes. We spent them talking about our jobs and everything related to them. People milled about us chatting and waiting eagerly for their name to be called. I spotted a young man seated at a nearby table taking off his hat while his girlfriend left for a few minutes. I couldn't see his face clearly from where I was sitting, but I could see what he was doing. He placed the hat down on the table with a box inside it. She came back, lifted his hat, and saw the box, opening it to find a ring. I could see her nod her head and respond affirmatively to his proposal.

"Your table's ready, sirs" a waitress suddenly told Dr. Powell and me. We followed her to a spot next to a bay window which gave us a splendid view of the wharf and the ships moored to the dock next to the restaurant. The sun was shining brightly, and I was feeling a mixture of emotions. I was excited to be talking to my mentor again but nervous about what he was going to tell me. Was he dying of a terminal illness? Did he get caught in some kind of scandal which he somehow felt compelled to share with me? All sorts of strange possibilities assaulted my overactive mind, and I couldn't calm myself.

"Mark, have you ever thought about the possibility of time travel?" Powell asked me.

I sat quietly for a moment as I thought how to respond to the odd query. Was Powell suffering from mental problems? That was another possibility for me to contemplate.

"I, uh, don't think about it that often," I stammered. "Makes for good entertainment in the form of books, movies, and TV shows. That's as much as the concept is worth, I'd say."

"I think you're wrong on your last point, sonny. I've been involved for the past six months with a team of people who are proving that time travel is a scientific fact and not fiction."

I looked around to see if anyone was listening to our conversation. No one appeared to be.

Powell laughed at my action. "Don't worry about listeners. The specific details of this project are being kept secret, but the project itself is a matter of public record. You got your phone with you? Look up Galveston College government project for this year."

I did as he said, and Google produced a list of articles on various government projects being conducted at the college over the past several years. "Which one do I click on?" I asked Powell.

"The article that talks about a particle beam accelerator device."

I did so and found an article that talked about an accelerator device that was being used to transport things in unique ways. My memory kicked in. "I remember this one. Looked boring to me. A bunch of scientists working on ways to transport particles or microscopic something or rather. Didn't seem to be me like they got past the theoretical stage. This is what you're talking about?"

"Yes." Powell relaxed and leaned back. He had the air of a man who had just confessed an indiscretion to his wife and was feeling both relief along with hope of forgiveness. "The project is real important, and several people have become involved. The article mentions the possibility of time travel. You probably didn't get that far. Everyone is thinking the same way you are. It's boring stuff for techno geeks and nerds who need to get a life. That's exactly what we want them to think. If anyone were to hear us talking about it now, they wouldn't bat an eyelash because they think we haven't really achieved much of anything. We have." He paused for a moment. "Perhaps I'm being arrogant by saying we. I haven't done much. I signed up and went back in time for just a few hours whenever they sent me. Never a long trip."

I did a double take as I tried to make sure I understood what he was saying. "You went back in time?" He grinned in response and looked me straight in the eye while nodding with confidence. I knew then that there were only three possibilities: he was telling the truth, he believed what he was telling even if it wasn't the truth, or Dr. Powell was a skilled liar on a par with an antisocial. I remember learning about lie detection in a psychology class I took when I was a college student. The teacher spoke extensively on the subject and showed us films. I got to watch nearly an hour's worth of footage of people lying, some convincingly and some not. I do not claim that I can always tell when people are lying. I don't think anyone can. Yet I knew that Dr. Powell was showing the facial expressions and body language demonstrated by the people in that film that were either telling the truth or the absolute best at deception.

"Okay,"—I reacted nervously—"what makes you so sure you really traveled back in time? How do you know it wasn't just a hoax being played on you?" I also wondered about the possibility of him hallucinating, but I didn't express that thought to him.

"I considered that myself," he replied calmly while looking away for a moment. "One of my colleagues passed away a few years ago. Heart attack. As soon as they proposed to me that I could travel back in time, they asked what time period I wanted to go back to. They allowed me a choice. I laughed because I thought the same thing you're thinking right now. I believed they were playing a trick on me. So I immediately asked for a time when the colleague I mentioned was still alive. I knew that I would thereby prove that it was a hoax. I gave them a specific date which I knew was before his passing. If my time-travel journey worked the way it was supposed to, I would see him. I thought I had them in a situation where they couldn't possibly get away with tricking me. I was smart enough to not tell them why I wanted to go back to that date. I told them nothing about my colleague's death. I made up some nice-sounding explanation for why I picked that specific date. I didn't want them to have the opportunity to find a look-alike who could pose for him. As soon as I arrived in the time before he died, I went to his office. He was there with the door wide open. Alive and well." For the first time, Powell looked as nervous as I was. Then, like an actor getting back into character after a brief lapse, he relaxed again and started describing his experience. At this point, I was definitely concerned about Powell. Was he taking drugs? Or did he have some kind of physical problem, like a brain tumor?

"They sent me back. I didn't think it would work. I was sure it was a sham. I chuckled all the way to that man's office. Then I saw his name next to the door. I froze. I looked through the open doorway, and he was there. I knew it was him. He didn't have a twin brother or close relative that resembled him. I actually double-checked to make sure. There was no way the people who sent me back could have found someone to imitate him on such short notice. They couldn't have possibly set it all up as a hoax, especially since I told them nothing about my plans to go to the man's office and see if he was there. He said hello to me and asked if there was anything I needed. I did my best to stay calm, but he noticed that there was something weird about the way I was acting. I made up an excuse. Told him that I recently received bad news about a close relative in poor health. He offered condolences, and I left. I felt like I was going to faint the whole way back to the drop-off point where the scientists pulled me back to the present."

I sat silently and ate my food as if Powell just told me the weather. I couldn't fathom what I was hearing from the man. I was excited and nervous at the same time. I knew that I had to hear more. It would have taken a gun pointed at my head to get me away. I felt enthralled with what he was saying because I so wanted to believe he was telling the truth. I had been fascinated with the concept of time travel for years, had read books on the subject, and was more than willing to pursue it. My answer to his query about whether or not I thought of time travel was what I told people to keep them from thinking me a hopeless romantic. I always feigned indifference to the topic of traveling through time or at least tried to act like I wasn't too fascinated with it.

Powell broke the silence. "Are you interested?"

"Excuse me," I responded. "You're asking me right now if I want to join in?"

"Yes," he said with a dead serious look on his face. The jovial expression that he had been showing was temporarily gone.

"I might have to think about it." I looked back at him. Once again, I was trying to play it cool and not look too eager, like a person interacting with a real estate agent who doesn't want to let on how much they want the house that's for sale.

"Of course, sonny." Powell chuckled. "I've given you a lot to think about. Let me give you my mobile number and email address so you can get in touch with me." He reached into his wallet and pulled out a small card with the relevant info printed on it. It was one of those cards they give professors to hand out to students. "Call or contact anytime."

The meal went on with the two of us conversing about everything but the time-travel experiment. He talked about his teaching job, and I talked about mine. I offered to pay, but Powell insisted on picking up the tab. We shook hands in the parking lot and went our separate ways. I drove home in an absolute daze. I suddenly remembered what the comedian George Carlin described as vu jà dé, the opposite of déjà vu. You have an experience so unique, bizarre, and unprecedented that you know it has never happened before. I could recall a few times in my life I had experienced it, and this conversation with Powell was the latest.

I got back to my small, modest home and tried to relax by watching TV, but nothing that was on could distract me from what had just happened. Should I sign on or stay away? I had no idea what to expect. What if Powell was simply mentally ill and merely thought he had traveled through time? That would explain why he was so convincing. A man who thinks he's telling the truth will often show the same body language and physical responses as a man who actually is.

If Powell was having mental problems, wasn't I obligated to inform others, like his employers? Perhaps I needed to gain his trust by playing along with him and then hopefully make him realize that it was all in his mind. Then an idea occurred to me. Of course! Why hadn't I thought of it earlier? Powell and the other people at the school were playing a trick on me and using deception for their experiment. If I went to the school, I would be put through an odd ritual or routine, and my reactions and behavior would be recorded. This was like the 1960s experiment done by Stanley Milgram. Participants were told to administer electric shocks to other people by flipping a switch. The purpose of the experiment was to see how many people would obey just because they were told to do. However, the other people were never actually being shocked. That was where the deception came in. No one was physically harmed. I had nothing to worry about. Powell was sane, and all I had to do was play along with him and do as I was told. I chuckled and breathed a sigh of relief. There was always the possibility that Powell and the others might decide not to use me when they realized that I had figured out a hoax was being played on me. I didn't mind that. It would be interesting to talk to them about the nature of their experiment and what they were trying to do. Perhaps I could even describe it in my class someday.

I picked up my phone, found his number on the card he gave, and sent him a text. I told him I was interested. I then sat and waited, feeling like a man on trial waiting for word that the jury reached a verdict. The verdict came. My phone made a noise indicating I'd received a text.

I picked up the phone and checked the sender. It was Powell.

"Glad to hear," the text read. "Come by tomorrow morning at about eight. My office is room 201. See you then!" I put the phone down and asked myself if I was crazier than he might be.

I went to sleep not long after and dreamed I was in a scene of the 1960 George Pal film adaptation of *The Time Machine*. I was in the machine trying to get back home when I was attacked by the Morlocks swarming around me and clawing at my face.

**2**

I DROVE TO THE COLLEGE campus the next day feeling a mixture of emotions, nervousness and excitement being prominent among them. Was this just a prank? Would I find out once I got there that Powell was part of some reality show that involved playing practical jokes on people? I could just imagine the host walking up to me with a microphone and a big plastic smile on his face to tell me that I had been suckered for the entertainment of millions.

The drive to Houston was pleasant but uneventful. It didn't take long for me to find the college I attended or the building that I knew Powell's office would be located at. I parked the car and sat there for several moments that felt even longer. Immediately my mind went back to when I was a student and constantly going to Powell's office to ask for help with an assignment. I laughed at the memory of how awkward I was in my late boyhood and how patient Powell was with my frequent interruptions of his office work. I got out of the car and walked slowly toward the entrance, feeling like that shy college student I was before.

I walked to Powell's office thinking he might not be there. He was. He saw me at his open door.

"How are you doing this morning? Nervous?"

"You really need to ask?" I replied with an eyebrow raise.

"No." He laughed. "Don't expect that nervousness to ever go away quickly, but the trip is quite safe. Remember the last time you had to travel by plane? How you felt when the plane hit turbulence? That's about what you can expect when we send you back. Let me take you down to where the machine is so I can introduce you to the scientists who make it happen. You'll also meet several other people hired for their historical expertise on the time periods we send people to."

We walked down the hallway till we got to the elevator and took it down to the basement. I had heard people talk about how the floor below ground was used for a variety of tests, studies, and experiments; but I was never sure if all the stories were true or not. I had attended college a long time ago when people were more likely to communicate in person than via the internet. My college classmates told one tale after another about what went on in the lower depths, as the basement of that particular building was jokingly called. By the time I graduated, I was so convinced that people were trying to one-up each other with ghost stories and yarns about what happened in that basement floor that I no longer took any of it seriously.

Could I have been wrong to dismiss everything said? It seemed I was about to find out.

We stepped off the elevator and into the place I had never been but only heard about. It wasn't really creepy or scary, much to my relief. The first thing I saw was a long, wide hallway with doors on each side and fluorescent lights spanning the middle of the ceiling. People were walking about talking to each other in low voices.

"Follow me, Mark." Powell led me to a room on the far left. I looked around at the faces of the people, expecting them at any minute to all turn to me and tell me this was all a joke. It didn't happen. They acted like they didn't even notice me. How many other people had walked this hall for the sake of this strange journey that I was now contemplating? I hadn't agreed for certain or signed anything, but I knew I had taken one small step closer. A man on his wedding day couldn't have been more nervous or excited as I slowly walked that long hall.

We walked into the room, and that's when I saw it. The machine that I somehow instantly knew would be the means for me traveling back in time. It was a large plastic cylindrical enclosure easily big enough to accommodate two people. The plastic was mostly clear like glass, but there was hard plastic on the sides of the box that was colored a light beige. On the gray plastic mat floor were two pairs of blue footprint outlines spaced so that a person could easily stand with a foot on each outline while in a casual stance. There was a black boxlike device on the top of the machine with a red light on it, so I assumed it was some kind of laser pointer. There were thick electrical cords going through a metal tube attached to the side of the machine. The cord went up the tube and over a cross beam attached to the ceiling before going down and into another smaller gray metal machine which had its own set of cords which ran along the floor to a series of computers at a set of desks.

"I take it you only want to send two people back for each trip?" I asked. "I see two pairs of footprints painted on the floor of the cylinder."

"That's our routine for now," Powell answered. "There's enough room in the machine for two people. Once we get a budget increase, we'll build a larger machine that could easily accommodate several people in the same instant. They've sent a lot of subjects all total since the creation of the first prototype several years ago. Some of the subjects have gone more than once and to different time periods."

"They actually want to sign up more than once?" I shook my head in wonder. I remembered when I was a child going on a roller coaster ride with a friend who was braver than me. She rode the roller coaster ride several times before our parents told us we had to go. Once was enough for me. What would my family think of me doing something like this?

I had a hundred questions I was tempted to ask Powell, but just then I saw a man in a lab coat walk up to us.

"Good morning, sir. Are you professor Mark Allen?" He spoke with an English accent that made him sound like a character in *Downton Abbey*. His thick brown hair was quite dark without any gray in it, but I could tell he was older than me. His face had the hardened look of a mature man in his mid-fifties. He was about my height and build.

"That's me." I shook the extended hand.

"I'm Dr. Peter Cartwright, and I'm here to tell you everything you need to know about our strange experiment. I don't want you to participate in this shindig until you are fully informed." His manner relaxed me and made me want to trust him.

A tech person wearing casual clothes walked up. It was a young woman, and I noticed that one distinctive thing about her was her badge hanging from her neck in plastic. It read, "Finney Series One Tech Assistant."

"Pardon me, Dr. Cartwright," the lady said. "We're getting some negative biofeedback from the person we sent back to 1950s. Their vital signs indicate they are getting nervous. I believe this is the one we told to investigate acts going on during the civil rights movement. I suggest we extract them."

"Good idea," Dr. Cartwright replied. "Let's extract the poor bloke now. See what they can tell us about what they saw concerning Jim Crow."

"Wait a minute," I said with genuine surprise. "You can track the vital signs of the people you send back?"

"Absolutely, Mark," Dr. Cartwright answered. "We have ways of tracking our subjects via electronic devices placed on them which each send out a kind of GPS signal and also monitor their heart rate, breathing, blood pressure, perspiration, and so forth. We've got tech people stationed at our computers to monitor their movement. The computers can show the person's location on a screen map. If their vital signs indicate trouble, we have them back in a jiffy."

Dr. Cartwright's words gave me a better feeling of security. I might be like a child walking through a dark room, but I would have people watching me while I was doing it.

"How about we find a place to sit comfortably and have a few drinks," said Cartwright. "You can call me Peter, by the way. I'm not real big on formality. Let me tell you all the basic info, show you the paperwork, and let you ask questions until you are out of breath. I've been through this procedure several times, so I've probably heard just about every query you can possibly imagine. I have a bet with your friend here that if any subject asks me a question that stumps me completely, I have to pay Powell twenty quid... I mean bucks, excuse me."

I liked Peter's sense of humor. He made me want to open up to him completely. We found a kind of sub-room with a wall that was half-glass. We all sat at a long desk in the middle of it. This desk had the distinction of being one of the few surfaces in the whole place not loaded down with electronic equipment. All I saw was a lot of papers stacked up in various piles.

"All right." Peter nodded at us. "First things first. These time-travel experiments have been going on awhile now, but we're not releasing a ton of information to the public. We don't want to tell people that we can travel back in time when we can't prove it, thereby making ourselves look like bloody imbeciles. Proof is the hard part, especially in this day and age. If we show people photographs or film footage, it's not enough. It doesn't take Steven Spielberg to do that much. Anyone with the right abilities and enough money can easily create fake photographs and fake film footage. We've got to figure out a way to do something that makes people realize that we had to have sent someone back in time in order for that deed to be achieved. We think we have it. Are you with me so far?" I nodded my head.

"The machine is called the Finney. I and my colleagues invented it and have made extensive revisions after we created the first prototype. The name has to do with an author of a time-travel book that I read a long time ago, in case you're wondering. It could easily be compared to a modern electric car. We've noticed that there are limitations to the machine which restrict what we can do with it. It needs more power the further you travel through time. For example, if you wanted to go back to yesterday, that would be like driving your car a few miles. If, however, you wanted to go back to the medieval period, that would be like driving about one thousand three hundred miles."

"Like that time I drove with some college buddies from Boston to Memphis to visit Graceland," chuckled Powell.

"I'll bet that was a fun trip," responded Peter. "And it used up a lot of gas."

"Did it ever," nodded Powell.

"How far back have you gone?" I was getting more excited and eager for details.

"The farthest back we've sent someone is 1836. We had them investigate the battle of the Alamo. Still some debate as to all the precise details of that famous incident. One of my colleagues is a friend of a pop singer who happens to be a fanatic about that incident and gave us some good ideas. I hope you don't mind if I don't reveal the singer's name. He probably wouldn't want to be associated with this project until we have the proof that what we are doing works."

"Of course," I replied. "So basically, you're telling me that the general public just sees what you're doing as a kind of odd study on the physics of time travel and nothing else?"

"Exactly. You can tell people that we're studying time travel and you won't be telling people anything they don't know. And if you tell people that we have actually sent people back, it won't matter to us. Without any evidence to support what you're saying, who would believe you?"

"That's it, Mark," continued Peter. "That's how it works. You can join us in this experiment and see the results yourself. You can't tell the public that we've done anything and expect to be believed unless we agree to back you up. What do you think? Still interested or would you prefer to walk out now, have a nice cup of tea, and go back to your regular life? You haven't signed any paperwork, so you're not obligated to anything. And if you decide after your trip that you never want to do it again, we respect your right to make that choice. We will pay you a reasonable amount of money for your participation. In fact, we can afford to pay you a hundred dollars just for spending one day listening to me and several others talk about it. What would you like to do now?"

I sat there and thought for several seconds which felt even longer. Was it getting warm in the room? Or was I just feeling the heat of my excitement? This didn't look like a prank being done just for someone's amusement. What they told me was consistent with what I had read on the net. I remembered reading the articles and thinking it was just a bunch of geeky scientists doing a lot of boring experiments with machines and computers. Now it looked like they were doing something different. I still didn't believe that they had achieved time travel. This was a trick being played on me. It had to be. They weren't really going to send me through time. They were going to put me in a situation that would provide the illusion that I was traveling through time. This was a psychological experiment being used to see how a person would react to suddenly being in an unusual time and place and having to adjust to it. Or something like that. I couldn't work out precisely what they were doing, but I would find out later.

I looked at Peter and said calmly, "You've got me for twenty-four hours. Let's get started on the prep work." Peter smiled in return and pulled a sheet of paper out of a manila folder on the desk.

"Sign the contract here, good man." He handed me a pen. "This paper shows you merely agree to participate in the prep work, as you call it. Complete all the stages and we give you the money for your participation. You then decide if you actually want to take the trip or not."

I signed the paper with a slightly trembling hand. My heart was beating a little fast, and I was definitely sweating, but I had no desire to turn back.

For the next two hours, Peter Cartwright gave me a kind of lecture on his time machine and how it worked. Powell told me he needed to do some paperwork in his office and left the two of us alone. I could understand why he didn't feel like sticking around. No telling how many times he had heard this info with other participating subjects. Why would he want to sit through it again?

I frequently asked Peter questions about the machine and how the process of time travel worked and any complications that might arise. Had the machine ever broken down? What kind of problems did time travelers typically have? Had they ever tried sending someone into the future? He answered all my questions with the utmost patience. I didn't think he had to worry about paying Powell twenty bucks on my account. He told me when he first started working on it and gave me an interesting history on all the prototypes that he and his colleagues had gone through before they finally had their first success. He told me about the subjects they had used and how they had been affected by their journeys. Peter talked to me about which time periods had been visited and the kind of information each traveler had collected. That was what each subject was called, a traveler. It seemed appropriate.

We eventually got around the to the subject of time paradoxes. I knew that people had been debating those for years. Can you prevent your own parents from conceiving you, because if you did, that would prevent you from being born and that would make it impossible for you to exist to go back in time and do that very thing.

"Okay," I finally said while rubbing my eyes and yawning a bit. "I feel a bit worn out by everything you've just told."

"Of course," Peter sympathized. "Would you like to take a break and get some coffee?"

"No, I would like for us to keep moving. What's next?"

Peter took a sheet of paper with a long checklist on it. "I have told you all the preliminary information I am required to for this stage, and you've obviously been a great listener. I am going to check that this part of the preliminary procedure is complete. Any more questions about the nature of the machine and the way time travel works?"

I couldn't think of any. Peter then told me that I would need to talk to historical experts who would tell me about the time and place that I would be sent to. They would tell me what I needed to know to blend in and not seem out of place to the locals. We left the room of the time machine and went across the hallway I had seen after getting off the elevator. Peter opened the door, and we entered a room that looked like a standard lecture room complete with a marker board, computer, and projector. Standing next to the lecture desk was a woman who looked like she was about my age.

"Professor Williams," Peter called out. She looked up from some notes that she had apparently been reading. "I have your next victim."

"Very funny, Peter," she responded to his jest. "And you must be Professor Mark Allen." We shook hands, and I nodded my head. Peter simply nodded and left the room.

"I assume you're the historical expert who's going to tell me what I need to know about where and when I'll be going?"

"Not sure I deserve to be called an expert, but thanks for doing so. Would you like to sit while I get the PowerPoint ready?"

"Sure thing," I replied and chose a chair that was at about the halfway point of the room.

I didn't want to get too far or too close.

"I'm a history professor, and I'm going to tell you what you need to know about Galveston in the year 1900."

For a moment I thought that time had stood still, which seemed appropriate for my situation. "Pardon me, did you say Galveston in 1900?" She nodded.

"You know something about that time and place?"

"Yes. I don't claim to have your historical knowledge, but I know that it was in that year the city was hit by one of the worst hurricanes in our nation's history."

"Yes. I have a feeling you'd be a good student for one of my classes." She maintained good eye contact and looked confident about what she was doing. I somehow sensed that she had been in the teaching business a long time.

"Do I need to address my teacher as Professor Williams, or can I be informal?"

"Of course you can be casual. Call me Carrie," she answered. Over the next several hours, she took me through the history of Galveston right up to the year 1900. Her presentation contained film clips, graphic displays, and a PowerPoint lecture. By the time it was over, I knew more about the city than many that lived there. I occasionally interjected with questions, and Carrie didn't mind having discussion and even debate on issues that related to the city's history. She made no attempt to hide the less-than-pure elements of Galveston history, such as its red-light district. I felt like a person watching a long epic movie and enjoying it so much they don't notice the time passing.

I noticed Carrie's appearance. Her curly red hair and pale skin made quite a contrast with her dark tweed coat that she wore over her beige blouse. She lectured with confidence and passion and did a good job of making eye contact. I could tell she was passionate about her subject. Anyone could have figured that out.

The lengthy lecture went by quickly, and Carrie said that she was done. We left the room and went across the hall to the machine room I had been in before. Peter was sitting at a computer with a strange graphic display on it that made me think of a radar screen on a plane's control panel. He looked up when he saw us.

"What do you think, Dr. Carrie?" Peter grinned. "Did Mark pass this stage of the orientation?"

"Absolutely, Pete." I noticed the way the two were so casual about names. The lack of formality reinforced my feeling and belief that this project involved a close-knit group of people who got along well.

"Mark did more than just stay awake," Carrie continued. "He asked questions and got us both into a lively discussion on Galveston's colorful history. Go ahead and check the next box."

"I will as soon as I'm done here. You can go home today, Mark. The other people that you need to meet with couldn't make it today. They got tied up with other jobs. We'll see you tomorrow at about eight, if you still want to continue with the orientation."

"Sure thing, Peter. I'll be here at eight sharp."

"Excellent!" He nodded to me and went back to his screen.

Carrie turned to me and said something surprising, "I've got some more things that I'd like to go over with you, but I can see that it's lunchtime. Would you like for me to tell you the details tomorrow, or would you be interested in me telling you during lunch? We each pay for our own meal, but I will let you pick the place. I can handle any restaurant in town. I like all kinds of food."

I liked the idea. It had been a long time since I had a meal with anyone but a coworker at the college where I taught. I didn't get out much, and my few friends sometimes expressed concern about it. My family definitely had teased me no end about my reclusive nature. Maybe this would be a good time to amend that.

We ate at a Japanese steakhouse in town. Carrie had a taste for sushi, and so did I.

"How did you get involved in this government project?" I asked while finishing off my spicy tuna roll.

"Simple," Carrie answered. "I've always been passionate about history and anthropology. My interest started in childhood when my dad told me yarns about the Southwest. He was a Texan, born and bred, who loved his home state. I studied a lot of times and places, but this area is special to me. This project gives us the chance to increase our knowledge about everything I've just said. I was contacted by Dr. Cartwright about a year ago. I've been assisting ever since. I've helped a lot of different time travelers. I can't really give you any identifying details about the travelers I've worked with out of respect for their privacy, but I can tell you I've worked with both men and women of varying ages and backgrounds. Many of them weren't as calm as you've been. They came back and gave us a lot of good info. It helped to answer a heap of questions that profs like me have been asking for a while now."

"Yeah, I'll bet." I sat there nervously and looked at Carrie. Her hair was a fiery red and her face was a bit freckled. She looked mature enough to be in her thirties, but there was a youthful quality about her persona that made her seem younger than her years. I knew that I could never expect Carrie's lectures to prepare for every aspect of this journey I was about to go on, but she had already helped me quite a bit. She made me feel like I would be serving a good and noble purpose by going back in time. There was something about her that I could not quite describe in words. The feeling was puzzling and reassuring.

"You read the material on time travel?" she asked.

"Well, yes…," I trailed off because despite having read it, I didn't totally understand it.

"You're having trouble with some of it?"

"Actually," I admitted reluctantly, "a lot of it."

She seemed sympathetic to my difficulty. "To time travel, you do not have to be an expert. Some of our travelers don't even try to understand all the principles. Let me hit some highlights quickly."

"Einstein's theory of relativity says time travel is at least theoretically possible. According to Einstein, approaching the speed of light slows time down. When we reach the speed of light, time stands still, and traveling faster than the speed of light takes you backward in time. Traveling at the speed of light would mean a trip from New York to LA would take about six minutes."

I was clearly impressed with her knowledge, and lacking anything else to say, I made a joke. "But it would take an hour to get through the terminal."

I immediately regretted the joke, but she laughed and then seamlessly continued. "The biggest problem with time travel is rules of cause and effect. If you cut your finger off, it's gone. If you travel back in time to stop yourself from cutting it off, it's still gone." I looked puzzled, and she continued.

"There are five paradoxes which science fiction writers have tried to creatively avoid and which science has ignored since we did not have time travel. The developments behind Finney changed all that. Do you understand them?"

"I've heard of them, I think. If you prevent your mother from meeting your father, you will not be born to go back in time, like in the movie *Back to the Future*."

"It is actually called the grandfather paradox," Carried corrected. "If you go back in time and accidentally kill your grandfather, then he will not give birth to your father who will not give birth to you. But if you are not born, you cannot go back and kill your grandfather."

"That is a paradox." My mind was grappling with the problem. "Has it happened?"

"Not as far as we know." Carrie answered, taking another bite. "However, some physicists on the project thinks it's not possible. In other words, you can't change history."

"Really." I had something else to think about. Then I added, "Have you tried to?"

"Definitely not! Another theory is a multiple universe; that you have now created an alternate timeline or entered a parallel universe." After a pause, Carrie asked, "Shall I go on?"

"By all means."

"The Polchinski paradox is a variation of the grandfather paradox, but it strictly involves motion."

"Huh?"

"If you shot a billiard ball through the wormhole back into the past so it hits its former self changing its trajectory, it will never make it into the wormhole in the first place."

My mind again swirled.

"We can skip it," she offered.

"Sounds good to me."

"Then we have the causal loop paradox. Everything has to have an original cause. Let's say in 2010 you missed an important meeting and did not get into Harvard."

"I wish I could have such a meeting. I doubt Harvard would even consider me."

"So," she continued, "you invent a time machine."

"Or borrow one from H. G. Wells," I interrupted.

"Precisely. I'm going to call the present you 'Now You' and the 2010 you 'Then You.' You use your time machine to go back to just before you missed the meeting in 2010 and confront the 'Then You' and get him to the meeting and get into Harvard. That means when the 'Then You' reaches the age you are now and becomes the 'Now You,' he will have to go back in history to get the 'Then You' to go to the meeting. It's an endless loop of cause and effect."

"I think I get that one," I said, but I wasn't exactly sure I did.

"Well then, there is the bootstrap. It's a kind of variation of the causal loop paradox. You take all of your savings and go back in time and give them to a younger version of yourself who uses it to make money so you will have it later on. So a cycle is set up. You are giving yourself money so you can make money that you can give yourself. The money has no origin."

"Next we have the 'Let's kill Hitler' paradox, which is a kind of a flip-flop of the grandfather paradox.

"Flip-flop?"

"In this case, you go back to right some terrible wrong. Killing Hitler, prevent the *Titanic* from leaving port."

"I get it, like warning the people in Galveston to get out of town."

The look on Carrie's face told me I should have kept my mouth shut. I had hit a soft spot. "Sorry," I stuttered. "I wasn't trying to question your ethics, I...I—"

"It's all right. The ethics of time travel haven't been established yet. Believe it or not, we have a group of ethics professors and a cleric debating the issue."

I was surprised. "They know about the machine."

"No, they think they have been hired by a university to debate hypothetical topics at inflated salaries."

"Go back to killing Hitler. It sounds like a good idea."

"Okay, you go back and kill Hitler. Which brings up a whole group of technical problems. You kill Hitler then, which means you have no reason to go back and kill Hitler now. Then suppose Hitler is replaced by someone worse like Stalin invading Europe. Remember that initially Hitler and Stalin were allies."

"Finally, though not a paradox, is the butterfly effect. A butterfly flaps its wings at Japan, and it causes something that affects something else that affects something else and so on, and it eventually causes a hurricane in Florida or Galveston." She stopped and watched.

"Those are complex problems," I stammered.

"That they are, but we don't have to understand or solve them today," she said with a smile.

"One thing I should tell you before I forget," Carrie interrupted my thoughts while she raised her glass to her lips for another sip of soda. "The crew should tell you tomorrow about you being assigned a mentor and guide who will arrive in Galveston in the year 1900 not long after you do. That person will eventually track you down and approach you to give you further instructions."

"Awesome!" I said with a slight grin. "My own babysitter. Do I get to find out ahead of time, or is it a no-no for me to even ask?"

Carrie swallowed her drink and looked nervous for a moment. "Well, they haven't officially decided yet who the person is going to be. You'll find out either shortly before or after you get back to your target site. Um, that's the term we use by the way. Target site refers to the time and place each time traveler is sent to."

"Of course," I responded. "Got to learn the lingo, don't I? Is there some sort of instructional manual I can read about this project as I prepare for my big trip?"

"There is. The mission objective people should give that to you tomorrow. They'll talk about your mentor and whether or not they've chosen anyone specific for that job. They'll tell you exactly what you do when you get to your target site and how much time you've been allotted to be at the target site. All that important stuff."

"Good to know," I responded. "Just out of curiosity, do you mind me asking if your family knows about what you're doing? I just wonder if friends and relatives of people involved are informed."

"They may know that we are doing a series of experiments involving quantum physics or mechanics, but they don't know that we're traveling through time. We don't want anyone other than people directly involved with the project to know about that important point. If you tell any of your friends or relatives, we'll have you dismissed from the project."

"I understand that," I told her. "Not that I have many people to tell. I'm an only child, and my mom died in a car accident when I was eight. Dad never remarried and died of cancer just two years after."

Carrie looked at me with a surprisingly calm facial expression, like an experienced psychologist or social worker dealing with a patient in a session. "Who took care of you growing up?"

"That's where my life story takes a good turn. My uncle Dave on my dad's side adopted me. He and his wife, Aunt Julie, showed me as much love as my parents did. They helped me get into college and paid for whatever my scholarship didn't cover. I owe them a lot."

"You said you don't have siblings. So your uncle and his wife didn't have any kids of their own?"

"No, they couldn't have children." I took a breath and looked at my watch. It was nearly half past one. I needed to get home and rest. Carrie and I paid for our meals separately and left the restaurant. We shook hands before parting company, and I drove back to my place.

# 3

I RETURNED TO THE COLLEGE the next day, and Powell took me down to the basement hall again. I was directed to a room on the left not too far from the elevator. There wasn't much in this room besides a door in one wall. I was greeted by a man and woman who quickly explained why I was there.

"Hi, Mark," the man said. He had a thick red beard and looked like he was somewhere between my age and that of Dr. Powell. "I'm Jeff, and this is Monica. We're just going to take your measurements for the 1900 style suit you'll be wearing if you go back in time. This shouldn't take too long."

On a small desk rested a set of books. One of them had the word *COSTUME* in capital letters on the cover. A sheet was next to it with a basic drawing of a person with blanks next to each part. I assumed this was a sheet used for writing down a person's measurements. Monica sat in a chair at the desk with a pencil ready to write down what Jeff said. Monica looked about forty or younger, I wasn't sure. Her thick, dark hair with a flawless complexion and slim figure gave her the look of a fashion model. Both Jeff and Monica showed the same calmness as other people that I encountered since I got involved, as if they were part of a project that had no element of strangeness to it at all. I kept having to remind myself that while the whole thing might seem bizarre to me, to them it had become routine and familiar. The man took a tape measure and put it around my neck while I stood still.

"His neck size is…," the man told the woman. She wrote down what he said on the sheet. "Sleeve length is…" And so it went until they had everything they needed. They told me that the suit should be ready for me the next day.

The next room I was sent to looked like an examining room in a hospital or clinic. There were several medical instruments, a weighing scale, and an examining bench just like I would see if I went to the doctor for a checkup. A man walked in and greeted me.

"Hello, Dr. Allen," he said. His hair was gray, but he looked young. I doubted he was past forty. "I'm Dr. Greg Smith, head physician and consultant on this project. We've got a team of physicians and surgeons who are in charge of dealing with the technology that goes into each person's body when they travel back in time. My job is to talk you through the process."

"Sounds good, Doc," I replied, trying to project a sense of ease that I didn't really possess. What were they going to put in my body? I was already nervous enough. This wasn't helping.

"All right," he said while putting his hands together. "First thing I got to tell you about is the electronic sensor that goes just under your skin. It will monitor your vital signs and send that information back to us along with a GPS signal that tells your precise location in time and space. When I put it on you, you'll probably feel like you're getting a tattoo. I'll use a mechanical insertion tool to insert the microelectronic sensor under your skin somewhere in your upper chest. Here's the tool I'll use."

Smith turned to a counter and picked up a tool with an electric cord plugged into the wall. Sure enough, it looked like a small metal tube inside a plastic part with an electric cord spiraling off it like what you'd see with a telephone.

"That will be done tomorrow, I take it?" I asked while swallowing.

"Yes," Dr. Smith answered with a firm nod. "If you give us a final confirmation that you are going on the trip, this will be one of the first things we do."

I thanked Dr. Smith for the info. We shook hands, and he told me I could call him Greg. He seemed to be quite friendly, like all the other people I'd encountered so far. He told me to head to the room where the time machine was to talk to Powell and the tech people. I promptly did so. Powell greeted me there.

"Let's take a look at what the tech people do, sonny." He took me to a row of computers set up not too far from the machine. People were there monitoring the flat screens. Several of them had their screen savers on, but one showed what looked like a GPS map with a dot that was moving across the screen at a good speed but then started to slow down.

"He looks like he's in a car driving down the highway on Bolivar Peninsula. He's stopping at the lighthouse." The young man saying the words was dressed in an appropriate lab coat and talking to a female also wearing one. She stared intensely at the screen.

"I know there was a movie filmed there in the late '60s during the time period we sent him to," she said. "I wonder if he's hoping to get an autograph from one of the actors." The young woman seemed to be quite amused by what was going on. Suddenly a much older woman stepped up behind the two others. A white lab coat, of course.

"That subject may be having fun," she interjected with a serious look, "but I hope he's completed his objective by now. He was supposed to drive to the nearby town and see if he could find any evidence concerning that unsolved murder at that diner. Both of you do remember that, right?"

The young man and woman looked slightly embarrassed, like students who just got caught goofing off when they're supposed to working on a classroom exercise. The man spoke first. "Yes, Dr. Trifimova. GPS signal indicates he went to the diner approximately eight hours ago. We're scheduled to extract him in the next twenty minutes."

I stood watching them as they stared at their screens, and I took a closer look at them than I had before. This was how they would keep track of me. They wouldn't be able to see or hear exactly what I was doing, but the GPS electronic sensor that they implanted in my body would apparently send out a signal through time and space to tell them precisely where and when I was. They had told me that already, but I was still mentally processing it all.

I was starting to get more and more excited. It reminded me of the time I interviewed for a job at the college I now taught at. When I sent in my application, I doubted I would even get a response. Then

I did, and it wasn't long after that I was interviewing for the job. Then they called me back to let me know they were very interested in hiring me. Each step of the way, I kept telling myself that it was too good to be true. Now I was feeling the exact same way. I still kept thinking I would wake up and find out it was all a dream; worse than that to me was the possibility that I was being played for a sucker. I would be so incredibly ticked off if that happened. I wanted it to be real. I wanted to commit to the project entirely and experience what those other people were experiencing. What should I call the others—test subjects, explorers, fellow time travelers? I couldn't quite decide what term I liked best.

"Dr. Trifimova, I had heard that the electronic sensor implanted in each, um, subject can also monitor your vital signs. Is that correct?" She turned at my question.

"It most certainly is," she responded with a mild Russian accent. "We can instantly tell your heart rate, blood pressure, perspiration, and other vital signs. If anything starts to change dramatically, all we have to do is use our computers to command the time machine to take a person back to our time."

"Think there's much chance of a machine failure?" I asked nervously.

"It can happen, yes." She didn't sound uncomfortable talking about it. "We have our own backup system down here, so we don't have to worry about a power outage, but there is a possibility that a glitch or technical problem could occur with the machine. It's not a cause for alarm, Mark. We will be able to send you messages via a small time machine which can make a copy of any printed material and send the copy through time and space to wherever we specify. It's a kind of quantum fax machine. We even have apps on our phone which connect us to it so we can transmit text messages and emails."

"I know it would take you too long to describe all the technical difficulties you've had to deal with since you started using the machine, but have any of them ever resulted in someone being stuck in a particular time for several weeks or months of their life or...or maybe longer than that?" I stammered nervously as I envisioned a time traveler having to survive in another time and place while they waited for the machine to be fixed so they could return home.

"No," she grinned slightly. "That's never happened. We have run through numerous testing and problem-shooting experiments to prepare for every type of bad-case scenario you can imagine. Our tech repair people are geniuses at fixing or replacing any part of the machine that gets damaged.

Professor Powell walked up. "What do you think, Mark? You look like you're getting interested. It's getting hard to resist the urge to say yes, isn't it?" He looked at me with a facial expression that I had never seen before. I couldn't quite peg it. It seemed to a strange mixture of joy and something else…sadness, regret?

"Pardon me for asking, sir," I said calmly. "Did you only go on one trip or were there other journeys that you signed up for?"

I suspected he was hesitant to tell me. "Yes, I did. Just one more. Why don't we sit down over there, shall we?" He gestured to a couple of chairs a few feet away from the tech people.

"I went one more time, and then I called it quits." He said it with a look of regret and lowered his head. "I volunteered to go back to May 23, 1934, to a road just outside of Gibsland, Louisiana. I wanted to see what happened to Bonnie and Clyde. They were gunned down by police officers in their car. There is still some debate as to the precise details. I watched it happen and then came back and reported what I saw."

My eyes widened when I thought about what Powell must have seen. The incident was well reported as being somewhat tragic and bloody. Bonnie and Clyde were infamous bank robbers (though most of their robberies didn't actually involve banks) who were stopped by police who then pointed their guns and filled the young man and woman with more lead than a pencil factory. Many people argued for decades afterward as to whether the officers had the right to do what they did. Did the officers try to give the two thieves a proper chance to surrender or did they simply execute them?

"What I saw was not pleasant," Powell chuckled at his own understatement. "Worse than what you see in some R-rated movie, especially because I knew that it was real. I felt like I was going to vomit by the time it was over. I got my info and headed back. It was so rough for me that I lost interest in going on another trip. At my age, it doesn't take much to make the old ticker I'm carrying go out. You've probably guessed why I didn't want to tell you this morbid tale before. I knew the other people would accuse me of discouraging you on purpose."

Powell took a breath and continued with his story. "I know that at this point, it doesn't really matter. I'm a good judge of character, and I can tell when a person is interested in going forward or not. That's a skill I acquired by hanging out with my dad when he worked in a used car lot. That man was practically psychic when he was around customers. He could always tell when they would buy. I don't claim to be as good as he is, but I can see how excited you are. I think you've already made up your mind. Am I right?"

I shook my head in amazement at how perceptive Powell was. He was absolutely right. Like a young man who finds out about the chance to serve in a war, I was eager to enlist. No gruesome or depressing story could stop me at this point, because all I could think about was the tremendous excitement I would miss out on if I refused. I would spend the rest of my life driving myself mad by wondering. I was going to sign up for going all the way. I was going to step into that time machine and see what happened. I was going to go on a journey that would be just as exciting as a trip to outer space. It was going to happen. I was going to do something that was far more adventurous than anything I had ever done in my somewhat boring and monotonous life. I looked at Powell with confidence and said the words that I knew would seal my fate.

"Tell whoever you have to that I want to sign up for the trip to Galveston in 1900." Powell extended his hand to shake it. We shook warmly and left the building. I drove home feeling like I was going to burst out of my skin. I suddenly thought of what Macbeth says in the Shakespeare play before he commits the action that seals his fate: "I go and it is done. The bell invites me." There wasn't any bell literally ringing as I was driving home, but in my mind, I could hear one.

**4**

I RECEIVED A TEXT MESSAGE from Powell late in the evening telling me to arrive at about eight in the morning the next day. I had a hasty breakfast at home and headed out. My excitement mounted the closer I got to the school. I parked my car in the lot and turned off the engine. I sat there for several seconds which felt even longer. My feelings defied easy description. Like a bipolar person with mood swings, I had been bouncing back and forth since the previous night.

I entered the building and went down the basement room. The elevator doors opened, and there was Powell with several other people standing with smiles on their faces. Carrie was there too. I felt like a man on his wedding day.

"How you doing this fine morning, sonny?" Powell greeted me.

"I'm feeling…well, not sure what to say." They all chuckled at my response. How could they not know how I felt? How many times had they been through this with other subjects who served as time travelers? The people in charge of this project had probably seen every type of reaction imaginable. I wondered if they had ever had one change their mind at the last minute.

"Well, Mark," said Powell. "There's some final paperwork for you to fill out in a room over here." He gestured toward a room to my right. "We'll give you as much time as you need to go over it and sign and date each part. Then you'll go to the doctor you talked to yesterday who will implant the electronic sensor in you that tracks your movements by precise date, time, and location as well as monitoring your vital signs. After that, you'll put on your costume and then head into the room to step into the machine. You ready to get this party started?"

"As ready as I'll ever be," I responded. I wasn't too nervous. I stayed calm as they led me into the room where a person in a lab coat was waiting for me with the paperwork laid out. They explained it to me very clearly. I read each sheet and put my name and the current date at the bottom. The forms really did look like what I might read if I was signing up for a standard job. I read where it said what my salary would be for participating in the experiment and also where it stated that if I told anyone that I had traveled through time, the company would not support me or support my disclosure to the press or media. The message was literally being given to me in black-and-white: you tell anyone that you really went back in time, you're on your own. Good luck getting anyone to believe you.

The part that was new to me was where it said that I would have to await further instructions when I got to my destination. This wasn't just a paid vacation. I had a specific objective which would be revealed to me later. The contract did tell me that I was to check into the Tremont Hotel, a well-established place for visitors founded in 1839. The original building was destroyed by fire in 1865. A new one was built in 1872, designed by architect Nicholas Clayton. That four-story structure was demolished in 1928. I was going back to September of 1900 when it was still in existence. It was one of the buildings that survived the great hurricane of September 8, 1900. I knew that was one of the reasons I was being sent back to 1900, since it didn't take Sherlock Holmes to figure out why 1900 was chosen as my time of destination. I chuckled at my thought of the famous fictional detective whose exploits were first published in the *Strand Magazine*. One of Galveston's historic districts is called the Strand, and I would be seeing it in all its Victorian splendor.

My instruction forms also included information about my contact and mentor. I read a basic description which told me to go to a restaurant in Galveston where a table would be reserved for me by my "sister," who in reality was my mentor under cover. She was apparently about my age, and I noted the brief physical description. That, and her first name, was all I knew for now. I could easily understand why my mentor was posing as a relative. It would give us an excuse to interact with each other without people in 1900 jumping to the wrong conclusion about why we were together. The alternative would be for she and I to pose as husband and wife, which might make us both a little uncomfortable.

I signed all the forms and handed them to the tech person in the room. He told me to go to the room I had been to before where I encountered the same doctor. He had me remove my shirt and then took out his tool and implanted the sensor. The procedure was done in less than a minute. If I'd had a tiny tattoo inked on me, it probably couldn't have been done any faster. Next was the changing room where I met with the clothing experts who showed me my authentic 1900 sack suit, along with a pocket watch and a bag with a handle appropriate for the year. The bag had already been filled with various items I would need for the trip: money appropriate for the time period, toiletries, clothing items and accessories, etc. I went into the bathroom attached to the larger room and changed. I looked at myself in the mirror. It was me, but it wasn't. I was no longer a twenty-first-century man but a man of the late Victorian period. I stepped out, and the people looked at me approvingly. The suit felt more comfortable than I expected it to. I wore a dark brown coat with light brown pinstripes and four buttons on the front. My pants had the same color and pinstripe pattern and a button fly rather than a zipper. My hat was a brown derby. The shirt collar was what took some getting used to. It was stiff and big and restricted my neck movements. My tie was dark brown with a large knot. The shoes were brown patent leather dress. The man and woman observing me said that I might need some practice moving around in the suit. I did a few practice walks through the room, and the man gave me good instruction in how to stand and show appropriate posture for a gentleman of the time period. He told me that there was nothing else for him and his assistant to give me and wished me luck. Only one thing left.

I walked to the room of the time machine, carrying my bag with me. I opened the door and there it was. The machine was ready, and the tech people were all busy performing their various tasks. One tech person looked at me and walked up.

"Hello, Mark." It was a young man I didn't recognize. "I'm Larry Duckworth. I'll be guiding you to the machine and telling you what to do." He then proceeded to do just that, like Pat Sajak guiding a participant to the board for the final challenge on *Wheel of Fortune*.

"Just step there where the footprint markings are on the floor," Duckworth said. "Tech crew, how we doing? Everything ready?"

A woman in a lab coat responded with a grin. "Everything's good to go. Give us the word, and we'll give the computer command to activate the Finney." She looked back at her computer as the other tech people focused on their screens as well.

"All right, Mark. I just need you to relax and stand still. Like you're posing for a photograph. I'm going to count down from twenty, and we'll have liftoff! Here it goes." Sure enough, Duckworth started counting down as I stood still and restrained myself from doing something goofy (i.e., jumping with joy or raising my fist).

"Seventeen, sixteen…," Duckworth counted, and I stood still and looked at the room. The tech people were looking casually at their screens. Duckworth was standing still and staring at me as he counted. I heard the machine making a slight buzzing sound. I looked at the metal box close to where I was standing.

"Five, four, three, two, one." Already? I must have been in a trance. Then it happened. Everything got bright white. I had to squint. Then it got completely black. I was no longer in the present. I was traveling through time. It was like floating in water. I didn't seem to be standing on anything. There was nothing for me to touch or hold on to. I was just in the space that I was in. There was nothing for me to even hear. Then, just as quickly as it had started, it was over. I saw the bright, white light again. Then it was gone. I was standing on solid ground in an alleyway. I was in some sort of city. But where and when? How did they move me that quickly? They couldn't have. Now I knew that the illusion part of the experiment had begun.

How were they doing it? Was this like a virtual reality program? It certainly was convincing.

I looked at what was around me. If I was looking at computer graphics, they were impressive. I saw brick walls on my left and right sides. I saw solid ground under my feet, and I saw an exit to the alleyway. I knew I couldn't just stand there. I had to move and do the things they had told me to do. I had been given specific objectives. I had to play the game and continue.

I took a moment to breath and then stepped out of the alleyway. That was when I saw it. The city of Galveston. It wasn't the Galveston that I knew and had become accustomed to. It was different, just as I was different because of my changed appearance.

How can I describe what I saw? I'll try. People were walking all about, and they were wearing the nicest clothes I'd ever seen. For a moment I felt like I was going to pass out. Was I dreaming? Had it actually happened? I took a moment to inhale and exhale and tried to remain calm. I suddenly remembered a time in my college days when I visited England with a professor. It was so surreal to me at first. The nation that I'd seen depicted in movies and TV shows and read about in countless books was there. I was in the place that I had fantasized about. Now I felt the exact same way. Galveston of 1900 was all around me. I knew that this couldn't be a set. No one could recreate the old city district of Galveston with such detail. Such a recreation would cost enough to bankrupt the most successful film company in Hollywood. Either the people in charge of the project had created a kind of fantasy image that seemed real to me or I had truly traveled back in time.

I started walking forward as slow as I could until I found a bench to sit down on. I looked around some more and rubbed my eyes. It was all still there. I saw old-fashioned buildings that were several stories tall. I saw men, women, and children wearing clothes that were authentic to the late Victorian period. A woman and a man walked past my bench. This was it. My first close look at human beings from that time period. I reminded myself that they were just normal human beings, not aliens from another planet. Yet I couldn't help but feel a strange thrill when they got near enough that I could see their faces and bodies. The man was wearing a dark coat and suit. He had a top hat on his head. The woman was wearing a long skirt that went down to her ankles and a tight-fitting white blouse with a brooch at the neck.

Then something happened that nearly made me jump. The man turned to speak to me.

"Pardon me, sir," he asked. I looked at his face. His complexion was pale, and he had a thick handlebar mustache. His hair was a dark brown that had a kind of auburn tint to it. He really did look like the stereotypical Victorian gentleman. "Would you happen to have the time? My pocket watch seems to have stopped." I like to think I did an impressive job of staying calm as I pulled my own watch out. Had the tech people set it to the time of day for my arrival in Galveston on that particular day in September of 1900? I certainly hoped they had, otherwise I was in trouble.

"Um, yes," I spoke awkwardly. I looked at my watch. It was ticking all right. I said the time was about half past one in the afternoon. I told the man that. He turned to the woman and started speaking to her in another language. Was it German? That's what it sounded like to me. The woman smiled at me and said, "*Danke Shoen.*"

"She said thanks," the man translated for me. "My wife comes from a German family that settled here a while back. She speaks a dialect called Texas German. Thanks again for the time."

"Kom mit mir, meine Frau," the man said to his wife. They both left. I sat there in a stupor. I remembered from my history lesson in the tech basement that there were a lot of Germans or people of German heritage living in Texas by the end of the nineteenth century. At one point, about a third of Galveston's population consisted of people who either immigrated from Germany or were children to those that had. I suddenly found myself wishing I had said "auf Wiedersehen" to them as they walked away. I was in too much of a daze to say anything. I felt like I was paralyzed with a feeling that was a mixture of fear and wonder. When did the tech people say they would extract me? They did say I'd get a mentor on this trip to help me out, didn't they? They also said they would monitor my vital signs to see how I was doing physically.

What were they picking up now? Was I having a heart attack? It wouldn't surprise me if I did.

I knew that I couldn't sit on that bench forever. I had to get up and move. I had to be brave enough to put one foot in front of the other and go to my assigned destination. I had to try to act like a rational human being, otherwise the police might grab me and have me committed to the nearest mental health facility. I knew what those places were like. Were the ones in the nineteenth century any better than the ones we had in the twenty-first? Of course not! If anything, they were probably worse. No telling what the doctors in those places would do to me, and they would be able to get away with a lot. The laws concerning the treatment of the mentally ill weren't that strict back in those days. If I did get committed, I couldn't possibly tell the psychiatrist the truth about who I was and where I was from. That would guarantee I never got out.

I arose and attempted to walk down the street of the Strand that I was on, feeling like I might as well be walking on the moon. I suddenly chuckled as I thought of that song by the Police, "Walking on the Moon," and could hear it playing in my mind. It would be about seventy-nine years before that song was released from the point in time that I was in at that moment. The people walking all around me would most likely be dead by then. That was when I thought about the type of music they would be listening to. Scott Joplin, perhaps? There was much for me to think about as I slowly and carefully made my way through the Strand and tried to remember the basic facts I'd been told about that historic part of Galveston.

It had been called the Wall Street of the South. It was the part of the city where great businessmen had made their fortune. It was where rich men and women went to see and be seen. I could see them now, but I could also see people who were probably far from rich. I saw men and women wearing clothes that were formal but also worn and dirty-looking. I saw children walking about with faces that looked like they hadn't been cleaned or washed in days. I saw men and women with strangely pock-marked faces that reminded me I was now in a time when there was no vaccine for small pox. No telling how many people I would see who were scarred by their bout with that disease.

I walked slowly at first and then picked up speed. I looked at the buildings, and they looked terrific. They would hardly qualify as skyscrapers, but they were of good size, and many of them had an architectural style that was definitely different than what I was used to. I guess *fancy* is the word I'm looking for, but I'm not sure that any word can describe how excited I felt when I looked at them. I wanted to take pictures, but I knew that wasn't an option right then since I had no camera on me. All I could do was look and enjoy. I did.

I couldn't stop for too long or I might block the way of other people. The city streets weren't too crowded. Galveston wasn't too big a city in 1900, but it looked about as busy as it would be in my time of origin. I walked along the avenue and started to think about where I was and which direction I was heading. I looked at the buildings for a while as I walked and then looked up to see if I could figure out the angle of the sun. It wasn't helping, because I was still in so much of a daze that I could barely think.

I stopped and looked around to see if I could find the sign of a building that I could use for reference. I saw a lot of signs but nothing that seemed to give me a clue. I walked some more, and people moved around me. That was when I mustered up my courage to stop at a bench and do the same thing that the man who talked to me earlier had done. I felt incredibly nervous, like a young boy mustering up the courage to ask a girl out on a date. I saw a person who I would ask for directions. Like many men, I was often hesitant to ask for directions. I was now asking for such from a man who did not even exist in my time.

The man sitting on the bench had the look of an old Southern gentleman with his gray hair, thin mustache, and elegant suit and cravat with stiff white collar. He looked up at me and spoke first.

"Can I help you, sir?" he asked kindly. "You look like the kind of fellow who could use some assistance."

"Indeed, kind sir," I replied. I could hardly believe what I just said. "Kind sir"? I normally didn't talk like that, but I knew that I was now in a time period when people would speak in a manner that would seem somewhat stilted to us twenty-first-century people. I had to speak appropriately for the era.

"I was looking for the Tremont House," I finally told the man. "I have heard my friends say such marvelous things about the place.

Can't help but want to give the place a good look and see if it lives up to its reputation."

"Oh, it certainly does, mister," the man replied. His Southern drawl was noticeable but not too thick. "I reckon it's mighty booked up right now. There's a lot of folks coming here now to see some exciting things. You keep walking the way you're going and you'll see the hotel on this side of the street."

"Thanks, sir." I nodded and held my left hand to my hat and tugged it down slightly while gripping my bag with my right. I could hardly believe what he said. I was near the Tremont Hotel. I was in the Strand on Church Street. The hotel would soon be on my right (according to what the man said), which meant I was headed southwest. I would get a chance to see it before the hurricane hit. That hurricane would hit soon, but I would be back to my own time before it got bad. The tech people could easily tell by their tracking sensor what spatial location I was in and what precise moment of time I was in. They were set to activate the machine and extract me before the storm became fatal.

I proceeded southwest slowly and then a little faster as I kept getting more and more excited. I had to calm down. If I got too excited, that would give the tech people incentive to do what I had just thought about. I walked along the street close to the buildings on the north side of it. That was when I saw it. I suddenly realized I was standing right next to it. I blinked several times to make sure I was seeing clearly and reading the sign right: The Tremont House.

There it was. The entrance was right in front of me. I walked to the door and opened it and stepped into the lobby.

Now I really did feel like I was going to faint. I had been inside the lobby of the hotel before, but that was in the twenty-first century in the new version of the hotel that wasn't opened until long after 1928. I looked around and observed the people. I turned my gaze to the hotel desk, where I saw a group of men wearing suits and derby hats. Women were walking around the lobby and looking pretty in their long dresses, big hats, and elegant hairstyles. The floor was marble and the decorations very fancy. Potted palms were placed next to Corinthian columns along with dark brown leather chairs. The lobby had the atmosphere of old-style charm and high class. Too good for a guy like me. Busboys and maids in black-and-white dresses moved around constantly as they attended to their jobs. I thought I heard the sound of a band playing ragtime music somewhere. Suddenly I heard two men talking about a boxing match.

"You hear about that colored boxer Jack Johnson?" A man talked with another while sitting in a wicker chair. "He's up against one of the best, and I'm hoping he loses."

"Can I ask how much money you betting this time?" The other man looked like he was about the same age as the fellow who spoke to him. Their suits and ties were practically identical, but I could tell them apart by their hair color and the fact that only one of them had a mustache. I wondered how many mustaches I would see before I got back home. It seemed to be a popular look in this time period, which might make it difficult for me to tell one man from another. In any case, the man who asked about Johnson had a handlebar mustache, and the other was clean-shaven.

"I'd rather not say," replied the man with the handlebar on his lip. He grinned. "People say that Johnson is rather bold for a colored man. Been seen courtin' white women..."

I didn't really listen to the conversation after that. I knew that another thing I had to get used to in this time period I visited would be people making the kind of remarks that would be considered blatantly offensive in my day and time. No telling how often I would hear both men and women making politically incorrect statements that would invite gasps of shock if they were made in the twenty-first century. I was in a different time, and it was the type of experience that was already making me feel like I was in a parallel universe. Like Alice stepping through the looking glass, I was in a world that corresponded to my world of origin but seemed like a distortion of it. How many strange similes could I possibly devise to describe my adventure? I didn't have time to think about it. I had to walk to the front desk of the hotel and see about getting a room.

The front desk was just as elegant and fancy-looking as the rest of the hotel. A man stood behind it with a fountain pen in hand as he looked over a sheet of paper in a ledger in front of him. His attention was definitely focused on whatever information was on that sheet. He showed an impressive ability to tune out the distractions of everything going around him as if he didn't sense them at all. I approached him nervously. I couldn't seem to get over my feeling of excitement and anticipation at talking to a person who actually lived in this time period.

"May I help you, sir?" asked the man as soon as I got to the desk.

"Um, yes," I stuttered. "Do you have any rooms available? Just for one person."

"We did the last time I checked," the man answered. "Let me look again." He took out a separate ledger and moved his finger down the page. "Ah, yes. We have three here with one small bed each. You did say it was just for one person, correct?"

"Yes, that's correct." I breathed a sigh of relief. The people who sent me on this trip had given me more than enough money to pay for a room for several nights. I wasn't worried about expense. The problem was that we all knew that I was going back to a period of time when it wasn't always easy to get a room in a particular place in Galveston. I had been instructed to try the Tremont and see if there was an empty room. I certainly didn't look forward to having to try my luck at some other place.

"How about room 312?" The man's query interrupted my thoughts.

"Sounds good," I answered. I paid the required fee, signed the register, and took the key. A bellboy came to my attendance and led me up the stairs to my room, after taking my bag and carrying it for me. I gave him a good tip and entered my place of solitude and rest. I looked around.

It certainly looked different than what I was accustomed to, hardly a surprise. I saw a rug on a hardwood floor, a wall covered in wallpaper with an elaborate design, and a small bed. That was about it. I turned to the wall and saw a switch. Did this room have an electric light? I quickly flicked the switch and saw the light attached to the ceiling come on. Of course it did. This was the year 1900 that I was visiting. Public buildings all over the world were being wired for electricity, even if most people preferred lighting their homes the old-fashioned way. I had to remind myself that I was in a time of transition. The Victorian world was drawing to a close and being replaced by the modern world of the twentieth century.

I walked to the bed and sat down on it. All of sudden I felt like I might cry out. I laid down to rest and found my eyes getting heavy. Did traveling through time have a jet lag effect on the traveler? I tried to remember all the information that the tech people gave me, but I soon fell asleep. No strange dreams this time. I just slept.

# 5

I AWOKE SOMETIME LATER. WHERE was I? When was I? Was I still in the year 1900, or had the tech people yanked me back? I slowly looked around and saw that I was still in the same room I was in before. Same hardwood floor and light bulb hanging overhead. Indeed, the bulb was the first thing I noticed since I was lying down on the bed and staring directly up at the ceiling. I got up carefully, not feeling particularly comfortable in my old-style suit. I walked around and thought about my objectives for going on this journey. I felt like I did on my first day of college teaching when I wasn't sure what to expect or how I should organize my time.

Like the novice teacher I used to be, I wasn't sure what to expect or precisely what I should do first. I decided to check the time. I pulled out my watch. The long hand was clearly on the twelve and the short one on the three. I had arrived at the hotel and checked in between 1:30 p.m. and 2:00 p.m. My nap had lasted a little over an hour. I wondered if the tech people could tell that I was sleeping since they could monitor my vitals. Probably so.

I left my room and locked the door behind me. Felt interesting to lock a hotel door with a regular key that I would have to be careful not to lose. The futuristic concept of a card sliding through a metal slot attached to a door was a long way off. The twenty-first century was more distant to me than a man's home country while he vacations in a foreign land. Further away than the earth while Neil Armstrong stood on the moon. I stopped my poetic mental meanderings and reminded myself to focus on my objectives. Like a secret agent, I had to keep moving and meet the lady who would be my contact and mentor during this strange expedition. Would it be a teacher or a technician? How knowledgeable would she be? Someone with plenty of experience, I assumed, since she was supposed to be guiding me through the process of getting by in an era of time I had never lived in.

I walked down the hallway of the floor I was on. I admired the carpet and the décor. I noted the painting hanging on the wall. Was it the work of a famous artist or someone not well known? It appeared to depict a man and woman dancing in a room with a plant behind them. The woman was in the foreground, and the man was behind her in such a way that his face was obscured. His dark, short-cut hair could be seen along with what looked like a formal suit he had on. The woman was wearing a white dress and appeared shorter than the man since the top of his head was clearly above hers. Would I get a chance to dance with a woman like that somewhere in this romantic city? I wondered. I went down the stairs into the lobby and took a moment to look around it. It was about the same as when I had walked in. A fine and clean lobby with elegantly dressed men, women, and some children. I saw a boy holding a ball which he clearly wanted to play with. A man who I presumed to be the boy's father or guardian was discouraging him from using the ball in a way that might cause damage to anything in the lobby or annoyance to any person there. Two women chatted with each other and seemed to be giggling at nearly everything they said to each other. They were obviously in a good mood. I was excited.

I wanted to tour the city for a while. My suitcase was in my room, but the money I needed to purchase items was in my wallet in my coat that I was wearing. I decided to go for a stroll. I left the lobby and walked out into the Galveston of a time that I had never before experienced.

I walked southwest down Church Street till I got to 24th Street and turned north to the area of the island near the water. This was the part of the city I had been to many times before in my own time. It was where the tourist trap stores and shops would come to exist in future years, long after the year 1900 that I was currently in. Right now the area consisted of warehouses filled with tough and muscular blue-collar workmen loading and carrying goods and products to and from boats. I also saw finely dressed men and women holding hands and linking arms. Like models in an outdoor fashion show, all the people seem to be not just walking but marching with an air of dignity and poise. Unlike most fashion models today, however, these people were actually smiling and looking happy. The men were mostly dressed in suits with ties while the women wore long dresses, fancy coats, and some interesting hats. The men's headwear mostly consisted of fedoras and bowlers.

I saw the horses and carriages going through the area. This was something I was used to seeing in my own time, since it was a tradition carried on for tourists with a taste for the old-fashioned mode of travel. Now I was in a year where such travel was a matter of necessity and not just being done for the experience. I knew from my studies that the automobile had certainly been invented by 1900, but I didn't see one at the moment. I did see a streetcar going through the middle of the street with men and women loaded on it.

I looked at the stores and establishments on the street. I saw what looked like a pharmacy/soda shop. I decided to stop in. Inside I found a black-and-white checkered floor and a counter with metal stools lined up at it. The man behind the counter looked exactly as I expected him to: handlebar mustache, dark greasy hair parted in the middle, and clean-shaven otherwise. His clothes consisted of a skimmer hat which he hung on a coat rack and a striped shirt with a white wing collar and a solid dark tie. I approached him with my hand going into my coat for my wallet.

"How can I help you, sir?" the man greeted me warmly.

"I'll have a Coca-Cola," I answered.

He served me one in a tall glass. "Five cents," he said. I handed him a nickel from a pouch placed in my coat by the people who worked on my clothes. They knew that since so many things sold so cheaply in the year 1900, there might be numerous times when I would need only a few coins to purchase something, and it would certainly be inconvenient for the people and for me to have to deal with so many coins in change.

I thanked him for the drink and walked over to a wooden table near the entrance. I sat down and looked through the window and enjoyed watching the citizens of the city walking to and fro. I had been informed that the Coke I drank might contain trace amounts of cocaine. I assured the historical experts I worked with that I would drink slowly and carefully while they monitored my vitals to make sure that I was not in danger. They would certainly use the machine to extract me if they sensed anything wrong.

I left the soda shop and strolled down the street. The weather was warm since it was still summer, and I was definitely feeling it in my suit and tie. I looked at the stores, shops, and establishments in the area. There was a wide variety of places in this part of Galveston, and I could see how the city had already become prosperous by the early twentieth century. I saw banks, restaurants, clothing stores, and just about every type of place I could expect to see in my time. Again resembling Alice after walking through the looking glass, I felt like I had walked into a world that was not completely different than mine but rather an odd reflection of it. I walked and walked for a long time and began to wonder what time it was. I took out my pocket watch and saw that it was nearly five. Had I really been walking around that long? I needed to find the restaurant I was supposed to go to meet with my contact.

I found the restaurant I'd been told to go to. I walked up to a balding man in an elegant suit standing behind a counter with a large ledger on it.

"Good evening, sir," he said. "Do you have a reservation?"

"Possibly," I replied, nervously. The man looked back at me as if he wondered about my mental state. I knew I had to give him an explanation quickly. "A lady was supposed to reserve a table for us both. She's my sister, Miss Allen. She told me she would reserve a table for us both at about this time. My name is Mark Allen."

The man relaxed at this and began scanning his ledger. I felt like I was in a repeat of the situation I was in when I checked into the hotel. Trying to look and act normal while in a situation where I wasn't sure about all the details since others had arranged things for me.

"Yes, Mr. Allen," he said with a grin. "I see that you do have a reservation for a table at this time. Let me call one of our waiters who will escort you to the main room." He called for a young man in a waiter's uniform who nodded to me and led me through the entrance into the main part of the restaurant. It was definitely what I expected, but that didn't stop me from being thrilled by it. A red carpet with an elaborate pattern covered the pale marble floor. Exotic plants in large pots flanked the way to the room filled with tables, many of which were occupied by people. The waiter led me to a table next to the wall where I sat and waited.

This was the moment I was anticipating. I really did feel like a man going on a blind date waiting for the lady to arrive. Who was she? The people in charge had given me a name and a basic description of her appearance. I hoped she would be kind and patient with me since this was my first time-travel job. I supposed that if she complained about my performance, there would be little chance of me being allowed this opportunity again.

A couple minutes passed, which felt even longer before the same waiter approached my table.

"Pardon me, sir," he said. "There seems to be a lady here who claims that she is your sister and wishes to dine with you."

"That's right," I said. "I was expecting her. Her name is Caroline Allen. Slim and about my height with dark hair."

"That's right, sir. I will escort her to your table." I grinned at the waiter's formal language. Was it just waiters and other professional people who talked that way in the year 1900 or did they all?

Not long after, I saw the waiter return with a woman walking next to him. At first I was distracted by the brown box she was carrying with her, but then I looked up at her face and observed it. "Hello, dear brother. It's been ages since we saw each other last." The woman had a big grin on her face and looked like she was resisting the urge to laugh out loud. I didn't blame her. I was torn between the urge to laugh and the shortness of breath I was feeling by being surprised. I felt like I suddenly had to remind myself to breathe normally and stay calm. I recognized my "sister" all right. It was Carrie. Caroline. Carrie. I just now made the connection.

"Hello, Carrie. Sit down and let's chat. We have all the time in the world."

"Exactly." She sat and placed the box carefully on the floor next to her as the waiter turned to us both. "Would either of you care for something to drink?"

"I'll have lemonade," she replied. The waiter nodded and turned to me.

"Um, I'll have the same," I said awkwardly. I wasn't even sure what beverages they served here. I wasn't too thirsty anyway. The waiter left and returned not long after with our drinks. We waited until he left before speaking.

"Well, dear sister, this is quite a surprise." I looked at the woman and did my best to stay calm.

"I've got another one for you. My legal name is Caroline, and I do go by Carrie, which is the name I chose to use with you earlier so that you wouldn't suspect that I was your contact. I wanted it to be a surprise."

"I sense that I'm not the only one you've surprised like this?"

"Your hunch is correct, dear brother. I have been the chief mentor on these time-travel projects for a long time now."

"All right, Carrie. So what do we do now? Just basic sightseeing before the hurricane hits?"

"Not just that," she answered before taking a long drink from her glass. "I'd like us to observe a boxing match with Jack Johnson. He'll be in town to fight someone, and I think we could do a photo op with him."

"You're kidding. We're just going to walk up to him after the match and ask if he'll pose with us?"

"You got it. He's a popular boxer and local boy. You know he was born and raised here, right?"

"Of course," I said. "Well, what should we order for our meal?" I opened the menu placed in front of me on the table and ran my eyes down the list of choices: salmon steak; asparagus, broccoli, and various other vegetables; swordfish; sirloin steak; roast duck; quail; etc.

My mouth watered at the choices offered. Carrie had summoned the waiter.

"I will have the roast duck with seasoned vegetables. As for you, dear brother?"

"I'll have the salmon steak with potatoes," I told the waiter. The waiter made a formal bow and departed to give our order to the chef.

Carrie and I discussed several matters while waiting for our food. The time period and how we should behave toward each other since we were passing for brother and sister. Carrie stated her made-up history or fictional background for her cover. She was in Galveston looking for a husband, as so many women did in that time period after completing their education. My role as brother was to keep an eye on her and protect her virtue as our parents would want. I smirked at her description of what we would be doing until the team extracted us and took us back to our own time. After several minutes of that discussion, she took the box and placed it on the table in front of me.

"Take a look at it," she said with a big grin on her face. I did as I was told. It was a box, not too large, with a leather handle attached. I learned about this invention a long time ago. It was the camera invented in February of 1900 by Eastman Kodak which made it possible for people to take snapshot photographs, a radical concept for the time period. It quickly became one of the most popular cameras of the early twentieth century. We could easily use it to take pictures without arousing any suspicion or odd glances from the people in the year 1900.

"I've never seen one up close. Can I examine it?" She could probably tell how excited I was when I asked.

"Go right ahead, brother," Carrie replied with a wink. She didn't have to tell me twice. I grabbed the box and opened it to get a good look at this marvelous item of history, one of best inventions of the twentieth century. I wondered how Carrie obtained it.

"Did you get this from some antique dealer or...," I trailed off. She knew what I was about to ask.

"The tech people purchased it from a reliable source and then fixed it up so that it would work properly. I didn't purchase it brand new from a camera salesperson who lives in this time period. The people in charge have mixed feelings about us doing something like that due to ethical concerns. We certainly wouldn't want people sign-ing up for these time-travel trips just so they can grab a bunch of goodies, would we? If a time traveler has an objective that relates to a certain artifact in a specific time period, he or she may be allowed to retrieve it and take it to our time so that it can be studied and then returned after the study is concluded. In many cases, we simply send the object back through time by itself. We can do that with an object, as long it doesn't have more weight or mass than the average human being. Anything of great mass or weight places too much strain on the time machine."

I sat and listened to her description, utterly enthralled by what she said. I remembered how, when I was younger, I'd read stories about artifacts that went missing for long periods of time only to mysteriously reappear or be found by someone in bizarre circum-stances. Could this be why?

Carrie interrupted my thoughts. "So now you know the final detail of our assignment, what you and I are going to be doing together. We'll take pictures in the year 1900 and then take the cam-era back and have the film developed. No one will be able to accuse us of having the pictures photoshopped because we won't be able to touch them until after we get in a dark room and have them devel-oped in the old-fashioned way. As long as they develop properly, they'll show us in this time period and that will give evidence that time travel is possible."

"It won't be enough to convince everyone," I said wearily. "We'll still have to deal with the cynics who say we're playing an elaborate hoax and will never believe unless they do like we have and experi-ence it for themselves. I don't really have to tell you that, do I?"

"No," she said, with the air of a teacher who is patient with a slow student for pointing out the obvious. "However, it will be an important step. Sometimes it takes a really long time for a break-through in technology to catch on with the masses. Not because peo-ple are slow-minded, but because they have a healthy degree of skep-ticism caused by years of being played by con artists and hucksters. Ironically enough, in a certain sense, it's good for us if not everyone believes. We don't want to be flooded with requests from people who all want to try it out. Neil Armstrong and the other astronauts successfully landed on the moon, but can you imagine what would have occurred if a long line of amateurs had tested their luck after he came back?"

I nodded my head at her insight. I could clearly see how this whole project was being run by sophisticated people who had considered many variables and issues associated with the concept of time travel.

The food arrived, and I dived in. I noted that Carrie took a moment to pray before her meal. She closed her eyes and paused for several seconds.

"What did you pray for, if you don't mind me asking?" I queried.

"That we do well on this assignment and make it home safe," she said while looking directly at me. She had the look of someone who had just the right mixture of humility and confidence. Was that because of her faith? I wish I could understand.

"Well, I'm certainly not against the idea that there might be a higher power willing to help us out."

I grinned at the thought while hoping that I didn't offend her by making it clear that I wasn't part of her religious group. I knew that now was not the time for me to create tension by arguing with her about anything. Carrie had shown me that her knowledge of this time and place was impressive, and I needed her navigational skills.

We eventually finished our meal, and I paid the bill with the money I'd been given. We walked outside. It wasn't dark, but the sun was clearly lower than it had been when I left the Tremont and began my tour of the city. I turned to her and paused for a moment.

I wasn't sure how to phrase my next question.

"Are you staying at the Tremont as well, or did you find a different place?"

"I'm at the Tremont. I need to get back so I can write up some progress notes, which I will hand off to another traveler who's scheduled to arrive to pick them up before going back to our time to deliver them."

"Okay, so I'm not the only person involved in this project. I'm glad to hear it."

"Yes, but you are the only person who's working under my direct supervision." Carrie looked confident as we strolled together through the area while people walked past us. I considered holding her hand or trying to walk arm in arm with her, but then I reminded myself we were posing as brother and sister, not husband and wife.

"Yes." I put aside my thoughts and responded to her statement. "I'm very flattered that you allowed me to work under your supervision. May I ask what led to your decision?"

"It's very simple. I read your profile before I lectured you. That's standard procedure when the team pairs a supervisor or mentor like myself with a new recruit. I'm not the first to be in this position, you understand. There have been others before me. I started out as a recruit just like yourself but then quickly rose in rank. I hope I don't sound like I'm bragging. You don't have to be a superhero or genius to attain my position. You may be mentoring a new recruit yourself before too long."

I immediately felt like rolling my eyes in disbelief. Me supervise another person on a time-travel journey? I would sooner consider running for president of the United States. I let Carrie continue with her explanation.

"I felt that you were the kind of person who would be a good choice for this job. I made my recommendation to the heads of the team, and they approved it. After we get back to our own time, you'll be asked to fill out a simple evaluation form. It won't take long. I'll then fill out a detailed report on your performance. It's not an evaluation where I say whether you were good or bad. Supervisors aren't allowed to do that. We have to give an objective description of all your principal actions during this assignment, and then the people in charge decide whether or not to allow you to take another trip, so to speak."

"Right. So what's my evaluation form going to look like? Will it be a bunch of questions like, 'On a scale of 1 to 5, with 1 being the lowest and 5 being the highest, how would you rate your supervisor when it comes to...,'" I trailed off as I saw Carrie looking like she was about to start laughing.

"I'm tempted to chuckle because your description isn't far off the mark. My evaluations by new recruits are usually positive, but if you don't want to work with me again, I won't take it personally."

"Well, it sure is going good so far." I looked at her, and she looked back warmly as we walked back to the hotel and strolled through the lobby before saying goodbye to each other. She told me her room number in case I needed to reach her and instructed me to meet her downstairs tomorrow at eight. She would then give me the details about where we would be going and what we would try to get pictures of. We parted company, and I walked up the stairs.

As I looked down at the stairs, I noticed the rug with a fancy pattern on it. I particularly noticed how it was kept in place. At the base of each step was a brass bar which ran from the left side of the step to the right. On both sides of the step, the bar was screwed into the wall. I reminded myself that I was in a time period when the vacuum cleaner hadn't been invented yet. Rugs and carpets couldn't be attached to the floor because then it would be difficult to clean them. They had to be held to the floor in such a way that they could be taken off the floor when necessary. The brass bars held the rug in place on the stairs and kept if from shifting under people's feet. The brass bars could always be unscrewed whenever it was time to take the rug up for cleaning purposes.

I went to my room and read a Victorian novel that I'd packed in my bag. Later in the evening, I got ready for bed. After turning out the light and laying down before closing my eyes, I thought, *We are brother and sister. I have to remember that when people in this time ask about us.* I didn't pray, but I hoped that the god that Carrie believed in would help us achieve our goal and get back to our own time safely.

# 6

I SLEPT PEACEFULLY THROUGHOUT THE night and awoke the next morning as the room filled with the light of the early sun. I was eager to begin the day and complete my assignment. I got up and washed my face with water from a basin that I filled from the tap. They did have running water in this hotel along with electricity. I had to remind myself that though I was in an earlier time, many of the amenities that I had become accustomed to did exist. I took out my straight razor and shaved carefully after lathering. My usual method was an electric razor, but I knew that wouldn't be an option for me now. I was reminded by the historical experts that clumsy use of the razor could easily result in a slit throat. I did the best I could and, to my credit, avoided cutting myself. I've never been able to grow a really thick beard like so many men can. At this moment, I wasn't complaining as it made my task easier. I looked out the window at the great city of Galveston and marveled at it. Here I was in a city that had a smaller population than it would in the twenty-first century but still looked just as grand.

I washed my hair quickly under the tap, dressed, and left my hotel room and went downstairs. The shampoo that I used was in a glass bottle that had been given to me for the trip. The glass bottle was perfectly appropriate for the time period, but it contained modern shampoo. If anyone in the year 1900 obtained the bottle, they would probably marvel at the strange liquid inside, which was why I had been instructed to make sure I kept it to myself. I was wearing the same suit I'd worn yesterday. I knew that I wouldn't be spending much more time in this new world of 1900. The people who sent me back said that my last day would be when the hurricane hit. The machine would then be activated to take me back to my own time period. I was glad. I walked down to the lobby and took a moment to look around. Once again, I was struck by the simple elegance and quiet dignity of the place. No advertisement signs or boxes of tourist brochures like you would see in the twenty-first century. No television set giving us the news. No people listening or watching clips on their smartphones or iPods. None of that stimuli which we are all used to being distracted by in our time. Just a group of people sitting or standing while having quiet conversations with each other. I'm not sure I can properly convey in words what a surreal experience it was for me. I relaxed and looked around to see if I could spot Carrie.

She hadn't arrived yet, but I saw men dressed in dark suits with narrow ties. The suits weren't all the same; I could see that now. I was seeing them in color, quite a contrast with the black-and-white photographs I was used to looking at. Some of the men wore dark brown suits while others went for solid black, and then there were those who wore striped suits. Many of the men had derbies and bowler hats on. Faces varied. I saw a few beards but mostly handlebar mustaches and thick sideburns on some. Other than that, they were clean-shaven. The women certainly looked distinctive as well. Their straight dresses went down to their ankles over dark-colored shoes or boots with pointy heels. They definitely had some big hats on, with plumes and feathers. I saw a few of them wearing straw sailor hats with a black or dark brown silk band around the brim. There were also some women wearing motoring hats with veils attached to protect their faces from dust when they went riding in an automobile. I noticed that some of the people had some scars or marks on their faces. I remembered thinking yesterday that small pox was a common affliction in this time period, its most noticeable effect being a marred complexion. Then I saw her.

Carrie was seated in a wicker chair next to a potted palm. She wore a striped skirt and white blouse with a small coat and a broach at her collar. She had a hat in her hand as she sat. She saw me and made eye contact. She stood up and walked toward me to greet me with a handshake.

"Dear brother, how are you doing this fine morning?" I snickered at her dramatic way of greeting me along with her volume. She was obviously speaking just loudly enough that others could hear. I still couldn't get over the fact that we were now living in time period when such speech was common. Well, I could match her.

"Quite well, good sister."

"I thought we might go to the location of the boxing match with Jack Johnson, after which we'll eat at Ritter's Cafe. I asked one of the employees at this hotel who informed me that many are going to it. I'm sure it will be the most exciting event of the day. Have you heard of this boxer named Johnson?"

She was of course staying in character when she asked that. She knew well that she had told me about Jack Johnson herself when we talked with each other back in our own time. He was one of the prominent historical figures she lectured me on in preparation for this journey. I took a moment to recall the information I had been given. Jack Johnson was a black American born in Galveston on March 31, 1878. He made his debut as a professional boxer on November 1, 1898. I certainly hadn't read any biography on him, but I had heard about him since my youth. Not only was he a strong and successful boxer, but he also got people's attention by being in intimate relationships with white women during a time when blacks and whites had to be careful how they interacted with each other. By the time he died, Johnson had been married to three different white women. He had also been arrested for violating the Mann Act, which prevented a black man from transporting a white woman across a state line.

Of course, not everything I was thinking of about him had actually happened at this point of time that I was visiting. In 1900, Johnson was still a bachelor and not as famous as he would be later on in the century. Carrie and I would be seeing him box and using our camera to get photographs of the event with us in the pictures. That was our goal, and we would only be given one chance to do it. That was something I had asked about before. I wondered if a time traveler was ever given a second chance to go back to the exact same time and place to do something. The people in charge assured me that it was possible but frowned upon due to ethical and safety concerns. I could understand that.

We left the hotel and walked down the street until we found a horse carriage with a man sitting at the front. He wore a dark suit with a top hat and had a white beard. I thought that he looked like a much thinner version of Santa Claus.

Carrie told the man which section of the city we wanted to go to, and we both hopped in.

The carriage moved forward not long after we were seated, and I took a moment to relax. I was eagerly anticipating seeing the great historical figure Jack Johnson. I recalled looking at pictures and film footage of him. Would he look the same up close?

Carrie sat next to me and looked to her left and then to her right in my direction.

"You're looking forward to this?" she asked.

"Are you kidding?" I responded. I took a moment to listen to the clip-clop sound of the horses' hooves on the ground. I enjoyed the warm weather as I looked down at my suit. "I understand that after this boxing match, the Finney will be activated. We'll be pulled back along with all our items."

"Correct," she told me. "The Finney is designed so that it not only transports people through time but small objects as well. Any object too big to fit into the machine would be untransferable. The tech people talked about someday creating a much bigger machine, but I don't know if that will happen. In any case, all of the items we took with us when we traveled back to this year can easily fit into the machine so they will go back with us." Carrie and I were both careful to never refer to the Finney as the time machine. We knew how dangerous it might be to refer to our time traveling around other people who might think we were crazy. Even though we knew that the man driving the carriage couldn't easily hear us even if he wanted to, we still had to maintain the habit of speaking in a kind of coded language so that we would never have to worry about what would happen if someone did hear us.

It took some time for the carriage to get us to the location of the boxing match, and my anticipation mounted with each street that we passed. I remembered the time when I was a kid and my uncle took me to see a movie at the theater that I had been waiting months to see. I was so excited standing in line. I was interrupted from my flashback as the carriage approached the sight. I looked through the side of the carriage and saw it.

It was a boxing ring on the beach. Countless people were milling around about it. I looked into a floating sea of derbies, homburgs, and bowler hats on the heads of men walking around in suits of varied colors. There were few women. That didn't surprise me. It might be common for women to attend boxing matches in the twenty-first century, but in 1900, it was considered improper for ladies in general. The few women who attended this match were either from the lower classes, which is why they would be looked down on no matter what they did, or the liberated kind. They were the ones who were fighting in the year 1900 for women getting the right to vote and do so many other things they weren't allowed to do without being judged by the men who dominated America in that period. There might be a few upper-class women attending alongside their husbands.

I also wasn't surprised the boxing ring had been set up on the beach. The laws about boxing matches in city limits back in those days were interesting: they couldn't be held on city streets or in public buildings. However, the law didn't apply to what was conducted on the beach. We got out of the carriage, and Carrie paid the coachman's fee while thanking him. The coach left us there. We approached the crowd. I could feel the heat real good in my thick suit and marveled at the people who wore such heavy clothing in summertime during this era we were visiting. No doubt Carrie was feeling nice and warm in her heavy period skirt and such.

We could hear the crowd making cheering noises and encouraging the boxers. I could feel the sand crunch beneath my fancy leather dress shoes. Then I saw him. Jack Johnson was moving around the ring like a dancer doing a strangely choreographed routine. He held his arms and fists up with the boxing gloves covering them. His face moved too much for me to get a long look, but I could see his features well enough as he darted to and fro. His bald head was smooth. His face had a nice symmetry to it which was accentuated by his bow lips. His dark brown skin was as smooth as his bald scalp and gave him the appearance of a sculpted statue. Johnson was smiling at his opponent and looking completely nonplussed as he circled the man he was fighting. He was a thin, white man with short-cut hair that was getting damp with sweat. He looked determined yet frazzled as he tried to punch Johnson, only to see him punch back with great intensity or effectively move away. Johnson could block every blow delivered and counter with the greatest of ease. He was like a fighting angel who seemed to practically float on the surface of the ring.

I heard the cries of some of the viewers at this sparring spectacle. Some of them yelled a racial slur at Johnson, letting him know that they weren't thrilled with his success in the fight. Others encouraged him: "Get him, Johnson!" "Give him a right hook!" "Go for a haymaker!" Boos and jeers rivaled the cheers while Carrie and I got closer and closer. Many people were no doubt betting money on this match and couldn't help being emotional about the outcome. Some of the men turned their heads to look at her. I guess I couldn't blame them. They barely glanced at me.

Johnson and his opponent suddenly got in a kind of wrestling grapple, with Johnson holding onto his white antagonist as the man kept trying to get one hit on the bronze boxer with the strength of an ox. I watched with eager anticipation as the two struggled against each other. The wind picked up slightly, and some sand blew against me. Some unpleasant smoke drifted my way. Many of the male spectators were indeed puffing away on thick cigars, cigarettes, and pipes. No telling how much smoking was going on in this year when so many people (including doctors) were not too knowledgeable about the dangers of tobacco use.

I couldn't tell how much longer the fight lasted. I seem to lose all sense of time as I watched, mesmerized, by the fight. Then it ended. Johnson knocked out his opponent, and the man hit the mat. The referee counted to ten, and the other boxer, his body glistening with sweat, lay exhausted until it was over. Johnson had won. The crowd erupted with noise, and I saw Johnson give them a big grin while he raised his two arms in triumph. He walked slowly from the ring to his supporters and the men who worked with him. One of the men, a short black man, handed Johnson a dark robe for him to put on. The man was wearing striped pants, a crisp button-down shirt with a brown bow tie, and suspenders. He also had a cap on his head.

Carrie and I got closer and closer to the ring. Many people were already moving away from the ring with disappointed looks on their faces. The boxer that Johnson defeated slowly crawled to the edge of the ring with the aid of his own handlers and workers who helped him and then raised him up as best they could. He put his arms around two who carried him away. He looked weak and tired. His hair was matted with sweat, and his eyes darted everywhere as if he was in a daze.

Johnson was stepping down from the ring and onto the beach. We saw him talk to the man in the striped pants and bow tie. The two of them were laughing and looking quite excited. Johnson was a lean man with a muscular torso who stood six feet tall.

"You fought good, Johnson," the man said. "Can't think of anything to correct. You didn't do anything wrong."

"Of course not," Johnson replied. "I made a lot of mistakes out of the ring, but I didn't make any in it."

My eyes widened as I heard Johnson's words. I had read that quote a long time ago. It was one of the things Johnson was known for saying. Here I was witnessing one of the most famous people in American history making of one of the statements that went down in books. I was witnessing it. I couldn't get over that. I took a moment to collect myself as I remembered that I wasn't just there to have fun by watching an exciting event. My job was to assist Carrie with one of our objectives.

"Pardon me, Mr. Johnson," Carrie called to him as she looked directly at his face.

"Would you be willing to pose for a photograph with me and my brother?"

Johnson jerked his head at Carrie. He kept his pleasant facial expression but combined it with a look of slight surprise. Was he accustomed to having people pose with him for a picture after a fight? Was any boxer used to that sort of thing back in 1900. After all, this was long before the era of the selfie. I stood still as a statue as I looked at Johnson's countenance. It really did look just like what

I saw in those many photographs I looked at, except now his face was in full color rather than black-and-white. His face, which had a curiously symmetrical quality to it, was pointed at Carrie before he turned to look at me. If I had been staring at an alien from outer space, I wouldn't have been more hypnotized by the sight of it than I was then. I held my gaze with the great man of boxing history.

He nodded his head. "Sure, lady. I don't see why not. Just don't get too close. I'm a bit sweaty." He chuckled at his remark. So did the other man.

I turned my head away from both men as I looked at the other people milling about. Some of them seemed rather casual or nonchalant about what we were doing while others glared and shook their heads. I had to remind myself that I was living in a time that was definitely post-slavery but hardly identical to my own in terms of relationships between blacks and whites. Some of the white people in the time might be very progressive while others would be just the opposite. Fortunately, for Carrie and I, Johnson was as casual about posing with a couple of white people as he was about boxing a white man in the ring. I also took a moment to remind myself that the Kodak camera was a relatively new invention in 1900, and many of the onlookers were probably fascinated with our use of it.

I handed the Kodak camera to the bow-tied man assisting Johnson who waited for us to stand together and get still. We all grinned while the camera flashed. We then shook hands with the famous boxer, and I took the camera back from the other man with a polite nod and thanked him. We walked away from Johnson and all the people around him as we strolled away from him and the ring. I took a moment to look back at the swarm of people dissipating. The fight was over, and we had achieved one of our objectives. Carrie and I had something else to do on the beach before we headed to Ritter's Café. This was the place that we had to get in and (most importantly out of) before noon. That's when it would be hit by the storm and demolished in a matter of minutes. We couldn't tell the people that. Carrie and I both knew that to do so might alter major events in history, which would have repercussions.

What we just did with Jack Johnson was something we could get away with.

"Look over there," Carrie said to me as she pointed away from the ring to the waves crashing on the beach. "Do you recognize that man?"

A man stood there and walked in our direction but not toward us. He looked like he wasn't in a good mood. His dark suit coat was over an equally dark vest. The man wore a crisp white dress shirt and dark black tie. His short-cut hair gave him the look of a military man. It was perfectly parted on one side. His bulbous nose and thick beard and mustache caught my attention next. The mustache had ends so pointy they'd be sharp enough to cut someone. His pointy beard had the effect of making the bottom half of his face resemble the lower part of the letter *V*. His graying hair was covered by the panama hat he wore. He was calm but not happy, a man distressed about something but trying to keep it together. I had seen his countenance in several pictures. He was the one who would always be linked to the storm. Some would even say it should have been named after him. I recognized him from the photographs I'd looked at several times. It was Isaac Cline, the famous meteorologist who saw the signs of the hurricane that would devastate the island city. As if coming into contact with Jack Johnson wasn't enough, we were now looking at the man who was part of our second and final major objective: the storm.

I was so stunned by his presence that I felt immobile. Carrie certainly wasn't.

She cried out to him, "Mr. Cline, may we have a word with you?"

He stopped, and his dark eyebrows got close together, the expression of a person who is genuinely surprised or perplexed. "Perhaps," the famous man responded. "What exactly did you wish to speak with me about?"

"I merely wanted to ask you about this weather we're getting today," Carrie replied with the utmost poise. I felt like I wasn't sure what to do next besides stand there mute. "My brother and I have been fascinated with the study of weather," Carrie continued. "We know you're a respectable and highly skilled meteorologist. Do you think any of us are in danger right now? We thought what's happening right now might turn into a noteworthy event in the history of your field."

I was tempted to roll my eyes at what she was saying. Would Mr. Cline think she was a mad woman or a harbinger informing him of what was to come? He looked at her for several moments as if mystified by what she just said and then answered.

"I'm not exactly sure whether this weather we are seeing right now is a cause for concern. Hopefully it won't be. Nevertheless, I am going to talk to as many people as I can and get the word out that it may at least be necessary to avoid the beach and shores of this island. I will be going to my office in the weather building now and possibly sending out a telegram to report this situation to others."

"Of course, Mr. Cline," she responded with a polite nod of her head. "One final request. Would you be kind enough to pose for a picture with my brother which I will take with my Kodak? He's as great an admirer of you as I am."

"Certainly," Cline answered with a look of slight embarrassment and possibly bewilderment. At this point in time, he was not as famous as he would become several years later and was probably not accustomed to interacting with fans. "Is that one of those new Kodak cameras?" Cline asked. Carrie nodded in response.

He and I stood next to each other while Carrie faced us with the camera. I stood close to him and tried not to look nervous. I could see the skies turning gray, which almost gave the day a wintry look. I could hear the crashing of waves on the beach and the strong winds. It would get worse soon. I remembered my history lessons well. Carrie took the picture, and I nodded in a friendly manner to Cline as he nodded back and tipped his hat. He turned and walked away from us both. Carrie and I looked as he marched away from the beach and receded into the distance; a historical giant of a man headed toward destiny.

We found a streetcar that would take us to Ritter's Café. The streetcar was loaded with men and women, many of whom were discussing the unusual weather. The water level was starting to rise, and people were wading through parts of the city.

Galveston was starting to resemble the Italian city of Venice. Carrie and I enjoyed looking around the city as the streetcar moved through.

The streetcar slowed to a stop at Strand Street. Carrie and I got off and stepped into the famous Ritter's Café, which we knew would be demolished by the winds of the hurricane in several hours. I felt as if we might as well be stepping onto the *Titanic*, but we could take comfort in knowing that we would avoid the terrible fate of many who remained until the end of the lunch hour.

We quickly found a table, and I took a look around. I saw wooden tables covered in clean, spotless cloths. Waiters dressed in fancy clothes with white dress shirts and black ties scurried back and forth among the dinner guests while they carried trays and plates loaded with crabs, lobsters, and large steaks. My mouth began to water as I thought about the fact that I still hadn't eaten yet.

"Waiter," Carrie called to a clean-shaven man who looked like he was nearing fifty but moved like someone half his age. "Would you be able to take our order and see that it gets to us fairly quickly? My brother and I have an appointment to keep, and it would be dreadful if we were late for it."

The waiter nodded and immediately took out his notebook to take our order. I ordered a steak and some potatoes while Carrie ordered some seafood. The man took everything down and went back to the kitchen. She and I sat quietly while I looked around to see if any famous people were here. I had once read a description of many of the men who were in Ritter's when it got hit, but I couldn't remember precisely when they arrived. We might have come too early to meet them, and we couldn't stay long enough to ensure that we did. That was the paradox. We might want to witness the famous historical event, but we couldn't do so without endangering our lives. Above our heads, on the second story of the building, was a print shop with several pieces of heavy printing equipment. When the hurricane hit, the ceiling of Ritter's Café would collapse, and the equipment would fall into the dining area, killing several men. At least one of the waiters would die. The one who took our order, perhaps? Suddenly I felt sad as I waited for our meal.

It came within about thirty minutes, and Carrie and I ate while trying to be inconspicuous at the same time. By the time we finished, more people were coming in as the weather worsened. The winds blowing into the café frequently lifted the cloths off the tables and got diverse reactions from the restaurant's patrons. Carried found money in a small bag that she carried with her and paid our bill. We left, but we both took one last look after we left the building. There it was. Ritter's Café in all its glory. We didn't need to wonder what it would like afterward. She and I had both seen the photograph of that.

We took another streetcar back to the Tremont and walked inside. She guided me to a couple of wicker chairs in the lobby, and we sat down and rested. Carrie sighed for a moment and then asked, "So what do you think? How did you like your first trip back in time?"

"I liked it a lot. Felt like a paid vacation. I might try again, if you think I'm up to it. It was a privilege to do it this time."

"Very nice of you to say that. We get different reactions from people that we recruit. I haven't been a supervisor too long, but I've worked with several men and women. Some of them really like the experience of time travel, and others feel that it's just too weird. They can't get comfortable, and I was hardly surprised that they didn't sign up again. We do have a psychologist on staff who studies the emotional and mental reactions of subjects who participate. He's actually categorized the different reactions and put them on a chart. He showed it to us once. We all noted that of all the people who have done this, there didn't seem to be too many lukewarm reactions. Either you really like time travel from the beginning or it makes you immediately uncomfortable. Sometimes you have an experience during a particular assignment that traumatizes you so that it's not realistic for you to keep making trips. Did Dr. Powell talk to you?"

"Yes," I replied nervously. I wasn't sure if I should talk too much about what he revealed. "He said that he did some time traveling himself until something happened that made him decide to opt out of doing another trip. He's a strong man. He probably handled that situation a lot better than I would have."

"Right," Carrie responded warmly. "That's something you must remember. Never judge yourself for wanting to opt out, as you said. These trips can wear people out after a while. We have observed that. It's kind of like being an athlete who never loses their love of the sport but just can't physically perform as well as they did when they started. These time-travel projects have been going for years, and there are many people who had to call it quits after so many trips."

"Has anyone died during a trip?" I asked quickly. Immediately I wondered if it was a good question to ask and if I would have been better off if I hadn't.

"No, that's never happened." Her reply was as abrupt as my query. I breathed a sigh of relief. I could see her smirking just slightly in reaction.

"What's the average number? Do you know?"

"Don't know if I could state an average, but the longest I ever heard of someone lasting is about twenty trips. Some guy who was involved when they were working on the first few prototypes."

I raised my eyebrows at the figure and wondered what it must be like to travel in time on that many occasions. Carrie interrupted my musing by giving me fresh instructions. "Be sure to pack up all your stuff and get ready to head back. It shouldn't be long before the tech people fire up the time machine and take us back. Obviously, if we go back here in the lobby, it would cause quite a stir as the people around us would see us mysteriously vanish. If you and I are both in our respective rooms, we can go back in private without being seen."

"Of course," I responded. "They can track our movement with those sensors they implanted to tell exactly where we are in the space of 1900."

"Correct," she told me. "You remember what the techies told you. The tracking sensors tell them not just precisely when we are but where we are. Which building, which floor, which room. I'm sure they gave you all the details. Simply go up to your room and wait a few minutes. You will see a bright light and then everything will go dark. You'll be back home soon. See you then."

"Thanks, dear sister," I addressed her by the title of her fake identity. She grinned. We stood and went upstairs to our rooms. I closed and locked the door behind me. I went to my bag and placed everything necessary inside it. I knew that even if I wasn't holding onto the bag, it would still go back. They had explained that to me. The time machine could retrieve any object it sent back as well as any person. They also instructed me to open the bag and check for messages from the time fax machine. I did so.

I opened the bag, and there was indeed a sheet of paper there. I wondered what it would possibly have written on it. Perhaps a word of congratulation on my completing my first mission or assignment, whatever it was called. I picked up the sheet and read the message printed on it:

Mark,

I am sorry to tell you that there has been a slight change of plans due to a technical problem with the Finney. One of its major components called the F37 Chrono Shield got fried by the Finney's last use and must be replaced. As I type this, a techie is checking the shelves of the stock room. If the appropriate part can be found, we'll have the Finney ready to take you and Carrie back not too long after you read this. If not, we'll have to hunt down the part from an outside source. That means you may have to wait until sometime tomorrow from when you are now to go home. I urge you to remain in the Tremont House where you will be safe from the storm. Keep your supplies with you, especially your camera with its undeveloped pictures. I will fax you another message the moment a tech tells me the situation regarding the F37 Chrono Shield. Good luck, and we hope to see you both soon!

Dr. Peter

I stood still and thought about what I had just read. How can I describe what I felt? I was afraid and excited (if it was possible to be both). Was there a chance I might actually get to experience one of the most dramatic events in US history? Was I going to live through the storm of 1900? I walked quickly out of my hotel room to see if I could find Carrie.

# 7

I FOUND HER STANDING IN the hallway looking in my direction. She had a sheet of paper in her hand. We stood and stared at each other for a few moments. I walked slowly toward her. I glanced at the sheet in her hand.

"Let me guess," I said. "You got a note from Dr. Peter sent via the time fax. It states that we're going to be here a little longer." We were obviously alone in the hallway, so I didn't worry about someone overhearing us. Otherwise, I would have used some sort of coded speech when talking about the time fax machine.

"Quite right," Carrie answered with a calmness that put me at ease. "This is no cause for alarm. We're in the right place for surviving the storm. This is where several people in Galveston sought shelter, and not one of them was lost. Best thing for us to do is gather our bags and supplies from our rooms and go downstairs to somewhere safe. We might also advise others to do the same, though I'm not sure they need to be told at this point. I've seen several already moving downstairs. I'll meet you in the lobby."

She didn't have to tell me twice. I went into my room and made sure I had everything I needed in my bag. I closed it before grabbing it by the handle and leaving the room. I tried to stay calm as I thought about how I wished I could send a fax back to the techies in the year 2019 where I was from. However, I wasn't in 2019. I was in 1900, a world where fax machines didn't exist at all, let alone the ones that could send letters or written material through time. That's why I couldn't have a time fax with me, since the techies didn't want to run the risk of that type of modern technology falling into the hands of anyone in the year 1900. The only items they allowed me to take on my journey through time were the kind that would have existed in 1900 and would therefore provoke no reaction from the people in that year. No, I couldn't send the tech people a message to tell or ask them anything. I could only wait for them to send another message to the inside of my bag for me to read.

I went downstairs and told the desk clerk I was checking out. I turned to my right and saw Carrie walking down the elegant stairway. She strode toward the front desk with poise in her 1900 costume.

The desk clerk was a man in his thirties with salt-and-pepper hair cut short and a pale complexion which gave him the look of a young Steve Martin. He filled out the appropriate paperwork and took my key.

"Weather is certainly getting a bit strong for mid-afternoon," the clerk said with a half-grin. "The sky is so dark you'd think it was night already."

"Yes, I quite agree," I responded. "I think it may be necessary for my sister and me to stay in the Tremont lobby or some other safe room until tomorrow. I fear that we are seeing the start of a terrible storm, and it will be necessary for us to stay here for safety's sake."

The desk clerk nodded. "Indeed, sir. I've heard people saying that the wind is getting stronger and the water ever deeper. I think this may turn into a day and night to remember for a long time to come."

I stayed silent as I marveled at how prophetic the man's words would prove to be over the next several hours. The clerk had hit the nail on the head. I gazed about the lobby as Carrie walked up to the desk clerk and went through a routine that was virtually a copy of what I had just done.

"My brother and I were excited about visiting this beloved city. Now we certainly have more than enough to be excited about. We're from Poplar Bluff, Missouri. We certainly don't have hurricanes there."

The clerk actually laughed in a manner that really did make me think he resembled the famous comedian. A relative perhaps? "Well, we Galvestonians certainly don't experience many dull moments on this island of ours."

Carrie and I took our bags and sat on a couple of wicker chairs in the lobby as we watched men, women, and children move this way talking to each other about what was going on and what they should do. Would the lobby flood soon? I wasn't sure how soon it would. I saw husbands speaking nervously to wives with boys and girls huddled around their big skirts. I saw men talking to each other and in some cases looking angry as they argued about whether to stay or evacuate. In one part of the lobby, I saw a girl holding a book that she was reading with rapt concentration.

The girl, a tiny little thing, was holding the book in such a way that I could see the title on the front cover. I also saw the illustration of a lion with a red mane against a green background who appeared to be wearing glasses. *The Wonderful Wizard of Oz* by L. Frank Baum, a story published in May of 1900 about a girl from Kansas named Dorothy who gets caught in a tornado and whisked away to the land of Oz with her pet dog Toto. I reflected a moment on how Galveston was about to be hit by a hurricane of such demonic force and terror that it would easily rival that twister.

Carrie opened her bag and looked in. Her facial expression suggested to me that a bag message was awaiting. Immediately, I opened my own bag and reached for the sheet of paper that I knew without looking would be there. I read it.

> I regret to inform you that we couldn't find a spare F37 Chrono Shield in our stock room. We contacted our parts suppliers, and a new F37 CS will be here no later than tomorrow morning. I see by our tracking sensors that you and Carrie are both in the lobby of the Tremont. By all means, stay there.
>
> Dr. Peter

The note was brief and to the point. My head fell back, and I looked up at the ornate ceiling of this grand hotel that would soon be the refuge for about eight hundred people trapped on this island of doom. Some estimates I'd read put the number of people in the Tremont during the storm to be as much as a thousand or more. They would be the lucky ones in this city of thirty-seven thousand. In less than twenty-four hours, that number would be reduced by at least six thousand.

Carrie and I sat in our chairs for a long time after receiving the message and tried to be as calm as we could under the circumstances. At least two hours passed while we watched people around us dealing with the increasingly nightmarish weather. Some people actually tried walking out of the hotel, only to walk back in moments later realizing how dangerous it was. Hotel staff moved to and fro while they assisted patrons of their establishment. Men, women, and children looked fearful as they came to grips with the realization that there would be no escape from the island for them that day. I suddenly recalled Dr. Peter talking about how one of the time travelers involved in the project had been assigned to go back to the Alamo in the 1830s when it was attacked by the Mexican army. I felt as if Carrie and I were in a similar situation now.

The only thing we could do was wait inside this fateful building until the storm passed.

There would be no deliverance for us until then.

I listened to the fierce wind outside. To me it sounded like the wailing of a banshee. I remember learning that, according to Irish folklore, a banshee was a spirit that stood outside a house and used its frightening voice to announce when a person inside was about to pass on. I certainly hoped that banshee wasn't calling for me. How bizarre it would be if I died in a year that passed long before I was born. I suddenly recalled the time paradoxes that Carrie and I discussed when we were both still back in our own time. That's when I almost did something I thought I'd never do. I was tempted to pray to the god that Carrie believed in and ask him to protect me and Carrie and keep us safe. Why not? Mark Twain once said that there is no atheist in a foxhole. Could it also be true that there is no atheist in a hurricane, and would it apply to a guy like me straddling the fence about God?

I looked over at Carrie and saw that she had taken out a small well-worn copy of a Bible from her bag. It was, of course, the appropriate kind for the time period: a black leatherbound copy of the Revised Standard Version translation, which was done in the 1800s. I looked at her as she opened it and started reading. I found the situation slightly awkward. I had no real religious convictions, and in the presence of someone who obviously did, I found myself unsure how to respond.

"You mentioned to me your Christian faith," I said, finally to fill the awkward void of silence.

Carrie nodded in response. "I suddenly feel like talking about it, given the situation. Would you be interested in a discussion?" I could see that her eyebrows were raised as she asked. I did not know how to respond and really wish she hadn't asked.

"Maybe," I responded hesitantly. I thought about her faith. To me, Christians were people who used their faith as a source of comfort. It was like a placebo effect. As long as you expect something to make a difference, it improves your mood. That was how I felt about religion in general for most of my life. My own religious experience had been minimal. My uncle was kind of a "once or twice a year attend church" type of Christian. As for myself, except for weddings, I stopped going as soon as I entered college. However, I was curious how she had developed her own religious beliefs.

"What made you want to be a Christian?" I asked as I looked at her.

"It's a long story, but I think we have the time," Carrie answered with a slight grin. She opened her Bible and took a moment to look at where she randomly turned to.

She chuckled slightly. I looked around to make sure we weren't being observed.

"Sorry," she said. "It's just that right now I'm looking at a passage that seems perfect for our situation."

"Uh, what passage is it?" I asked.

"It's the book of Ecclesiastes, chapter seven, verse fourteen. I'll read it for you: 'When times are good, be happy; but when times are

80

bad, consider: God has made the one as well as the other. Therefore, a man cannot discover anything about his future.'"

I was tempted to roll my eyes in disbelief at the fact that Carrie had randomly turned to such a passage. Coincidence or did she already have the passage marked?

"Good choice, dear sister." I knew that I had to be careful what I said and how I talked to her. She and I had to stay in character and pretend to be brother and sister until we were delivered by the tech people activating the machine and using it to extract us and get us back to the twenty-first century.

"So you still want me to talk about it?" Carrie's question interrupted my mental rambling.

"Um, okay. Tell me, sis, about your religion," I said somewhat sarcastically. I suddenly thought, would a man living in 1900 refer to his sister as "sis"? I wasn't sure, and I knew that I if I said the wrong thing to Carrie in front of the other people, I could blow our cover. I looked around, and it didn't look like anyone was listening to catch my use of a possibly anachronistic term. For what it was worth, I knew I could say "okay." That was a word coined in the 1800s. I had checked to make sure.

Carrie began her story of how she became a born-again Christian. I listened with divided attention while the storm raged about us. She got something she called "saved" when she was in her late teens. She wasn't raised in a Christian environment. Her family was respectable and had good values, but neither of her parents were particularly religious. The only time Carrie and her family went to church was for a wedding, a funeral, or for other specific purposes. She grew up hearing about God and the Christmas story, but to her, it was nothing more than that. Her parents never gave any reason to think otherwise.

Her story was interrupted by hotel staff telling everyone to move to a part of the hotel where we would be hopefully safe. It wasn't long before Carrie and I had to go with the other people of the hotel and had been led by the staff to a second-story room in the rear of the building that they felt was safest and for fear the lobby would flood. Carrie and I did not immediately start the conversation, to my relief.

However, we did start paying attention to other people. Carrie and I talked through the night and occasionally spoke to others. At one point (to my surprise), I struck up a conversation with a traveling salesman named Charles W. Law who told me he was going to write a long letter to his wife and children if he survived the storm. I knew that he would because I had read a book that mentioned him and contained the letter that he would eventually write.

By five o'clock, everything was black except for lanterns and candles. It was as if it was midnight with no moon. The wind seemed to grow stronger by the minute, howling, demanding to be let in. Occasionally there were crashes as if material was being thrown against the building trying to help the wind break in. Fear permeated the room.

During the early evening, some tried to doze fitfully. Even I found myself drifting off in the middle of a battle with the elements. I had heard of soldiers falling asleep on the battlefield. It always puzzled me until now. Sometime after six, I noticed that the wind was intensifying rapidly. I dozed again, as did Carrie. At one point, I woke up, and Carrie was talking to a couple next to her about God. I found myself listening to the conversation. The wife was extremely upset with her husband trying to comfort her but clearly upset himself. Carrie was arguing that God was a source of comfort even in a hurricane.

"But," said the wife frantically, "we could die tonight, and I would never see my loved ones again."

"Yes," replied Carrie, "I'm worried too, but I know I have eternal life in Jesus Christ."

Then the wife responded tearfully, "What does that mean?"

Carrie patted the woman's hand. "It means that like the thief on the cross, when I die, I will be with Jesus in paradise."

"But doesn't death scare you?" the wife asked.

"Billy Graham said, 'Death doesn't bother me. It's just the process that does.'"

I was startled because I realized that Carrie had just talked about a man who hadn't even been born in the year 1900. I could see from the expression on Carrie's face that she realized what she had said.

A moment of calm reflection passed over the woman's face. "Who said that?" she asked.

"Just a preacher I knew. His name's not important." Carrie glanced at me, and a look of understanding passed between us. Carrie continued to talk to the woman, who seemed to become calmer. But I began to think about what she had said, and it caused me to think. I supposed that death could be like having a tooth worked on by a dentist. It's not the loss of the tooth that bothers you. It's the pain that goes with it. I must have been deep in thought for several minutes, because when I looked again, Carrie and the couple were praying. I wondered what they were praying about. I looked at the wife and saw that she had changed. She was still looking nervous, but not like she had been before. Carrie was succeeding in getting the woman to calm down.

Carrie returned to sit beside me on the floor. "You certainly had a good effect on her," I said.

"I didn't," she responded. "The Holy Spirit comforted her."

"Who did what and why?" I asked her in the midst of my confusion. I had heard the term *Holy Spirit* but had no idea what it was or how it comforted anyone.

Carrie sighed, realizing my confusion. "Sorry, I used Christian lingo that only insiders understand. My fault. Let me keep it simple and start at the beginning." She paused as if she was trying to think of where precisely to start. She closed her eyes for a second. I wondered if she was praying.

"Okay, let me start at the beginning. God, as I see him, is an all-powerful, all-perfect being, who is very righteous. He cannot accept sin that is so common to the rest of us. Just as when you break a traffic law, if you're caught, you have to pay a fine or go to jail. Since God knows all, he knows when we sin. The fines have to be paid, and he paid them for us. His Son, Jesus Christ, died on a cross to pay for our sins. We must acknowledge and accept what he did for us to be forgiven of those sins. I know you may not believe some of this, but does the logic make sense?"

I nodded my head, because I was beginning to grasp her point of view. Carrie nodded and continued. "But we don't get the benefit of what he did for us unless we accept and acknowledge that we are sinners, that we have broken God's laws, but that we accept Christ's payment for us. When we do that, the Holy Spirit enters our lives and comforts and guides us. The Holy Spirit doesn't make the storm go away but gives us assurance or peace in the midst of the storm. I know that if the storm takes my life tonight, I will be united after death with Jesus."

I found myself puzzled. I saw Carrie as an extremely intelligent woman but one with a very strong faith. I had always thought Christian faith as a kind of placebo pill for the weak and insecure. Carrie was none of these. I think she could see the cross between puzzlement and respect on my face.

Smiling, she said, "We'll talk more later." To change my focus, I began to look around the room, and as I did, somewhere in the city it sounded like something exploded. These explosions, which I understood later, were buildings and houses simply disintegrating under the force of the storm. Missiles continued to pound against the walls of the building. Somewhere nearby, there seemed to be the sound of a building collapsing. At times, I thought I could hear human screams. I hoped I was wrong. The storm clearly was getting worse. I didn't know how we could survive if it continued. Mentally I knew the Tremont Hotel had survived and the people in this room had lived to tell. But the sounds made me doubt.

Here, where we were supposedly safe, there were fifty or so people, some adults and some children, spread around the room. Most of the children looked nervous or scared. Several were crying, as were some of the adults. One man a few feet from us seemed to be panicking. He was demanding of the hotel staff to find him a safer place. The staff did not seem to be paying attention as there was nothing they could do. Carrie got up and moved over to his side at about the same time as a minister did. The minister had an episcopal collar. He appeared bald and looked like he was in his late fifties. He was carrying a Bible. I started to join them but found myself feeling totally small and inadequate. I looked at my pocket watch and saw that it was about six. I could barely see. There were only a couple of kerosene lamps and a few candles lit in the room. Several minutes passed, and Carrie returned to my side on the floor. I looked over at the man. The minister was still talking to him, but the man didn't seem inclined to do anything foolish at this point.

"How did it go?" I asked.

"He's a mess, but I think he'll make it if he stays here," Carrie answered. "He threatened to run out into the storm and try to make it to a telegraph office. He doesn't realize how dangerous it's getting ready to be."

"Or how many people are going to die," I whispered to Carrie. "You all right?"

"Oh, I am," Carrie answered. "But what about you?"

I knew what she was really asking. She was wanting to know what I thought about what we had talked about, but I was afraid to start that discussion again. I put my arm around her, and she held onto my arm.

We sat silently. I watched the dynamics of the room. One man kept threatening to go outside and check. His wife held onto him tightly. Several others, I realized, were drunk, but it didn't seem to help them.

I heard the wind of the storm outside, and it was like a train roaring through the room. Carrie and I watched a young couple across the room having a heated discussion. We could sense the emotion, but we couldn't quite hear what they were saying. Strangely enough, it lulled us to sleep. It was later in the evening when I woke up again. I nudged her slightly. She stirred and looked at me and asked what time it was. The candles in the room gave me just enough light to see my pocket watch. My watch said it was a little after nine. At this point, the sound of the chaos was so great we could barely speak to each other.

Carrie shouted at me, "It's getting worse!" If I hadn't been looking at her lips, I wouldn't have caught what she was saying.

"We'll be all right," I said, trying to sound convinced. I wasn't. I found myself secretly wishing she and I could continue our conversation. I didn't trust God. I didn't believe in religion. I didn't believe in the church. But strangely I wish that I had. I suddenly realized Carrie and I were holding each other tightly, and we had been for several minutes. It was warm and comforting as the wind howled around us. We didn't attempt to speak again. We just continued to clutch each other. Sometime shortly before midnight, most of the candles had gone out. Only a few kerosene lanterns remained. A building very close to the hotel exploded, sending debris in our direction. And then another, and yet another. It seemed like it would never end.

The howling of the storm was intensifying.

# 8

FROM MIDNIGHT ON, THE STORM continued with howling blowing winds that crashed against the building bringing with them timbers and rubble that hit the hotel like cannonballs and bullet shots. It was interspersed with periods of dead silence followed by explosions and shrieks of people in terrible anguish. Inside the room, there were fitful dozes of sleep. The wood and timbers colliding against the building would wake us up with a jerk. Some in the room I don't think ever slept. Crying and shrieks would pierce the darkness of the room. Only two lanterns were now left on. Mercifully, the children fell asleep out of exhaustion. At times I woke up, and Carrie was laying on my shoulder. We held onto each other, and I found strange comfort in her nearness. One time, about four in the morning, I woke up to find her awake staring at me. She looked calm.

"The storm is letting up," she said. "The explosions have stopped, and only occasional debris hits the building."

And then in a strange, haunting, faraway voice, she added, "I don't hear screams anymore." She looked at the wall as if she could see through it.

I knew what she was thinking of but couldn't say it either. Around five thirty, everyone began to stir. There was a relief that had settled over the room. We all knew the same thing. We had made it. For a while, no one moved. Then a little after six, one of the men decided to go downstairs. He was back in only a few minutes.

"It's flooded," he exclaimed. Some of the staff smirked at each other. They already knew.

"It will go down," one of them said. Looking embarrassed, the man joined his wife and sat down on the floor. Carrie and I, noticing how we were holding each other, moved a little apart but not too far.

Looking at my face, Carrie asked, "Have you thought any more about God?"

It was a disturbing question because I had several times but didn't want to admit it. My immediate response was, "Uh…"

Carrie said nothing. She just watched me. To fill the silence, I blundered by saying, "You're putting me on the spot. I was never an atheist, not even an agnostic or a skeptic when it came to the existence of God. It's just something I didn't want to think about."

"Maybe in a foxhole is the place to think about," she replied. I did a double take as I realized that she was quoting Mark Twain and using the very quote I had been thinking about earlier.

"Yes, I was in a foxhole," I said in return. "If only I had faith like yours, but I'm the kind that needs proof."

"Like what," she said, "God intervening and the storm turning away?"

"That would have been nice."

"But then," she responded, "it wouldn't be faith. If you knew that you joined God's club and nothing bad would happen to you, you'd get all the money you wanted, you'd never have any sickness, then everybody would join that club. That wouldn't be faith, would it?"

"Yes, but it would be nice for everyone," I countered.

"But the world was marred by sin," she said. "You were given free will, and that free will gets you in trouble because you make bad personal and sinful choices. You do, don't you?"

I knew she was right, and it was because I knew my bad choices too well. I didn't realize I didn't have a retort, but I desperately wanted one. I thought she could see my dilemma.

"Just think about it," she said. "What time is it?"

I leaned my pocket watch in the direction of the nearest lantern. It took me a second to make out the time. It was a little after eight. One of the men made a brave attempt to go downstairs. It was still flooded. We all chose to wait. People talked and chatted with each other. Children told their parents they were hungry. That went on for awhile. I myself went down about an hour and a half later. Clearly, the water was receding. I was able to walk through the lobby with the water up to my knees. I only peered cautiously out the front door of the hotel which was now damaged. Large timbers blocked my view of the street. I turned and went back upstairs meeting Carrie coming down. She looked at me.

"I was worried," she said. We got back to the top of the room, and I announced to everyone and no one that the water was receding. One man quicky went by me and down the stairs. I heard him slushing through the water and boards being pushed away. Carrie and I stood at the top of the stairs, and he didn't come back. A woman across the room asked, "Can we go out now?" I looked down the stairs and then back at the woman who was questioning me.

"I'd wait another hour at least," I said. Carrie and I sat back down. Over the next hour and a half, several left. One wife and her children came back, but her husband went on.

Finally, about one in the afternoon, Carrie said, "Let's try it." The water in the lobby was still in puddles, but I was no longer trudging through it. Several of the boards had been moved back by people who had left already. We could step out of the hotel and out into the street, which was still somewhat flooded. We both looked up and down what had been Tremont Street. I can only describe my emotion as a cross between sadness and terror.

Carrie's face showed similar emotions. I realized my mouth was hanging open. There was little left of the buildings across the street. Timber, debris but nothing that could be identified as a building. I looked southeast on Tremont Street. Part of one building remained on a corner. Beyond that was what was left of a frame house. It had not been there the night before. The sun was shining down from a clear blue sky, making it easy for me to see the devastation and wreckage caused by the tempest we had endured.

"Which way shall we go?" Carrie asked. I looked both ways. There wasn't much difference. I suddenly realized there were bodies lying in the street. There was a group of men down at the corner of 24th Street trying to dig into the rubble.

"This way," I said, pointing toward the harbor. "This way is as good as any, and maybe we can go to the harbor." I don't know why I hadn't seen it before, but only a few feet in front of us was a naked body, the clothes had been torn off by the wind. I averted my eyes, but then I realized there were more bodies in the street. Carrie seemed unfazed. We stepped down into the street. The water was about a foot deep.

Carrie, who was holding onto my arm, stopped me and said, "This won't do." And looking directly at me, "Do not move," she said firmly. "I'll be right back," and disappeared into the hotel. I was confused but drawn by the men working. When I reached them, I could see what they were trying to do. From the pile of wood, bricks, plaster, and furniture I could hear faint crying somewhere beneath it. Someone was buried in there. I began to help them try to remove the timbers. One of the two men appeared to be a workman. The other was a man in a bowler hat and a suit similar to mine that seemed inappropriate for our situation. Slowly we removed lumber and brick, finally revealing an eleven- or twelve-year-old child injured and crying. Much of his clothes were torn off. We gently lifted him out, laying him on the pavement.

"We need to get him to a hospital," the man in the bowler said.

The other man said, "I'm not sure we'd make it. The roads are blocked." We looked at each other.

I realized another workman had walked up to my side and suddenly spoke: "They're setting up some first aid stations on corners, I heard."

Realizing it was Carrie's voice, I turned sharply, and instead of seeing her in her dress, I found a disguised Carrie in a pair of workpants, held up by suspenders, and a dress shirt with the sleeves rolled up. She was taking a picture. On her head was a cap with apparently her hair bunched up under it. Her lipstick and makeup was gone. She looked at me and grinned.

The two men, not noticing it was a female, started to pick up the boy on the ground.

"Let's see if we can wrap those wounds," Carrie said.

The one man found a shirt, which we tore into shreds, and wrapped the poor boy. The cloth was probably not clean, and we weren't experts, but it was an improvement. The boy seemed to slip in and out of consciousness but didn't respond to questions. The two men carried him off, as Carrie and I watched. I turned to look at her again with somewhat amazement in my eyes.

"The dress was not going to work," she said and then turned toward the wharf and said, "Come on." There were other bodies in the street, soaking wet among pools of standing water. Other survivors began to fill the streets. Everyone looked stunned and bewildered. A few were crying, but most just looked numb. I stopped after a while and turned in a circle as far as I could see. Very little had been left. Parts of building remained, and, in one or two cases, houses and buildings remained erect. But the city had been torn down. Some of the houses that remained appeared to be little more than skeletal wrecks. Something else that I noticed was a stench that was beginning to rise.

"I've seen pictures," Carrie said taking another picture. "I've read about the destruction, but you can't imagine it till you've seen it."

We moved on toward the wharf, stepping over bodies, only to find the wharf no longer existed. There were a number of people gathered where we were.

"I tried to count the bodies on the way here." I turned to see a priest standing a few feet from us. He looked at me. "I lost count," he said.

Carrie nudged me and pointed a little way away from us where people were laying the bodies of one child, a baby, and a mother. They were partially covered by mud. As I looked around, I saw that some sort of sea goose-slime covered everything. Another man spoke.

"The Harris home on Tremont was left standing," he said.

"The good houses were left undamaged," said by another man.

"No, they weren't," said by a woman dressed as if going to church. The hem of her skirt was soaked and torn. Her clothes suggested she was obviously one of the more prosperous people in Galveston.

"I hear there's another storm coming," another spoke.

Carrie spoke this time. "No, that's not true."

"Who did you hear that from?" the other one challenged.

"The weather office," Carrie answered. Carrie leaned in to whisper in my ear, "That rumor got started, and I know I'm not supposed to interfere, but the weatherman Isaac Cline will eventually stop it."

We turned and started walking back in the direction of the Tremont Hotel without speaking. Carrie took another picture.

"That's the last one in the camera," she said.

The destruction was more than you could comprehend. When we reached the Tremont Hotel, I stopped on the steps. Carrie paused and turned to go on in.

"I'll be in the second-floor room," she said.

I looked up and down Tremont Street. People were walking through the water. Some clearly injured. Already, the bodies were being stacked on corners. I don't know how long I stood there.

Finally, I turned to walk into the hotel and met Carrie carrying a tray coming back out. It had a couple of cups and something that looked like potatoes on it.

"Come on, let's sit on the steps," Carrie said. She put the tray down between us and handed me a cup of water. "Camera's gone. Vanished. I laid it down against a wall to get this stuff, and it wasn't there when I went back to retrieve it." I heard her, but I was staring at the water in the cup. It hadn't come out of a tap.

"It's semi-safe," she said. "Besides, we were mass-inoculated before we left."

"Where did it come from?" I asked.

"Out of the hotel rain-storage tanks," she answered. I drank. Tasted odd, but it was refreshing. I didn't realize how thirsty I was. Carrie was drinking out of another cup. I looked down at the tray. She picked up what looked like a peeled potato and handed it to me.

"Eat," she said. "It's not bad."

"Why potatoes?" I asked.

"Because food is scarce," she replied. "This was the best I could find. I think some of the hotel staff are hoarding it. We won't starve. We just have to stay hydrated. Drink plenty."

At that moment, I looked down the street. They were burning the bodies. Carrie noticed it too. I turned to her.

"If God is good, how could he allow this to happen?" I asked.

She leaned toward me. "When the world was marred by sin in the garden, everything was marred—humans' relation to God, humans' relation to each other, and humans' relation to nature. God has given a way to repair the relationship with him. And in the world to come, the environment will be perfect."

"What made you come to believe this?" I asked her.

"Nothing made me," Carrie said. "It was a choice I made when I heard God's message."

Just then I began to hear people singing. I had no idea where they were. I looked around, squinting in the bright sunlight, but couldn't find the location of the singers. I could hear their song well enough. It was a church hymn.

"Standing on the promises of Christ my King. Through eternal ages let his praises ring. Glory to the highest I will shout and sing. Standing on the promises of God. Standing, standing, standing on the promises of God my savior. Standing, standing, I'm standing on the promises of God." Their voices seem to get louder with each verse so that I could hear them clearer and clearer.

"Listen to that," Carrie said as she turned her head. "Probably one of the groups of people led by a nun or priest singing a song of praise in this difficult time. I'd noted in my studies that there were people who did that the day after the storm."

I looked at her as she looked back. I saw the wreckage and damage around us in my peripheral vision. I wondered how people could be so positive in such a tragic situation. What if they really did have something that I couldn't grasp? A special connection with God while I merely had an intellectual interest. Could I change that?

Suddenly it happened. Everything got brighter. Much brighter. It was a bright white light that made it harder and harder for me to clearly see anything around me. I knew that it wasn't natural. I saw people all around Carrie and me, and none of them were reacting at all to the mysterious bright white light. Why? The answer was obvious. They couldn't see it. The bright white light was only visible to me because I was the time traveler who was being drawn out of the time period and about to go through time from 1900 to the world of the twenty-first century that I was from originally. It was happening again. The process by which I had traveled backward through time was now happening in reverse. The tech people had activated the machine to pull me back to my own time. My time-traveling experience was over. I was going home. I felt like a man who had just had a long, strange dream that was now drawing to a close. Suddenly I got nervous. What about Carrie? Was she going back too, or were the tech people going to leave her there in Galveston of 1900 for a little longer? I hoped not. She had worked hard and been through so much. Besides, I loved her. That was the first time I had admitted it. I didn't just respect her as a coworker. I loved her for her strength and everything she had done for me. No! They couldn't leave her behind. If I got back and found they had, I would yell at them and demand they retrieve her as well.

My thoughts were interrupted when I looked at Carrie directly. I saw her looking around and squinting. She even placed her hand in front of her face. She was shielding her face from the light. She saw it too! The only way she could see it would be if she was going back like I was. Otherwise, she would merely see me vanish quickly. I breathed a sigh of relief.

"Carrie," I called. "We're going home!"

"We sure are," Carrie answered with the happiest look I'd seen on her face in a long time. "Here, hold my hand." She moved toward me and held out her right hand, and I extended my left to grab it quickly just in time before the flash of light extinguished itself. Everything was gone. The people, the city of Galveston, you name it. All was black around Carrie and me except for a mysterious faint light which made it possible for us to barely see ourselves as we traveled through the strange ether that seemed to surround us as we went through time from 1900 to 2019. This was like it had been before when I traveled back, except this time I had someone to literally hold my hand as I went back home. Immediately I thought of a song by the Beatles and laughed. It was a strange time for laughter, but I couldn't help it. As was true the first time, the travel back made me feel like I was floating slowly through dark water. I began to relax and breathe easy. Then it was over. A bright white flash of light again, and I squinted before shutting my eyes completely. Then I slowly opened them.

There it was. The tech room. There they were. The tech crew all gathered around and looking directly at us. Some were standing. Some were sitting at computers and desks. They were all obviously pleased to see us. I looked around for several seconds which felt like much longer. I touched myself with my right hand. I was intact all right. I was safe. I was alive. I was home. I turned to look at Carrie. She was there.

She looked back. Then she did something she hadn't done in a long time. She laughed. So did I. We then did something we had never done before. We moved closer to each other and hugged. We both laughed and embraced and held on to each other as if we were afraid that one of us might drift away. I felt like crying. Maybe she did too, but I didn't want to ask. I just wanted to enjoy the moment and rejoice in the knowledge that we were safe and sound. Our journey was over. The danger had passed. We let go of each other and looked around at the tech people who were staring back at us. Some of them were chuckling. I looked down at my clothes and then looked at Carrie. Good heavens! No wonder they were amused. Neither one of us looked our best.

My suit was stained, dirtied, and torn in places. Carrie's masculine attire looked interesting. She removed her cap, and her long hair fell out from underneath. We both started chuckling. In the midst of our laughter, one of the tech people walked up to us. It was Trifimova.

"Welcome back, you two," she said warmly. "Why don't you both take some time to rest, relax, change clothes, and do whatever you need to do. One of the crew members will take you to the rooms where we have your regular clothes stored. We can debrief you later and talk about the results of your mission."

I staggered away from the machine and tried to walk. I felt like I was going to collapse. Carrie ran to me and put her arm around me to help me.

"How about you lean on me and we'll get you to the room where your stuff is?" I nodded in agreement. She was more stable than I was. That embarrassed me a little, but why should I be surprised? She had done this before. Her experience had no doubt strengthened her so that she could handle it better. I swallowed my pride and allowed her to help me to the room. I felt weak, but I had enough strength to make it. Carrie led me to the restroom where my clothes were waiting for me.

"Take your time, Mark. I'll be waiting when you get out." She left me there. I changed my clothes slowly and awkwardly. My muscles felt stiff, and it took a while. When I finished changing, I looked at myself in the mirror. There I was. The regular Mark in his modern clothes. My old self again. I sat down on the toilet seat and paused for about a minute, which felt like a little eternity. My thoughts raced. Would I do this again? It was exciting, but I wasn't so sure I was up for it. I could sometimes be a tough critic with myself, and I just wasn't sure if my performance was good enough. I supposed I would have to let the people in charge be the judge of that.

I got up and walked back to the tech room. Within seconds of entering the room, everyone there turned and saw me. They actually started clapping and cheering. They made me feel like a triumphant actor taking a curtain call. I made a mock bow in return, which got more than a few laughs in response. I was feeling on top of the world. I walked to the conference room and opened the door and walked in. Sure enough, Carrie was there in her regular clothes with her hair combed. So were several others seated at the desk. I saw an empty chair and sat down at it. It was now time for the debriefing. I was ready.

Dr. Peter was the first to speak. "How are you doing, Mark? You've been through quite an adventure. You're glad to be alive and safe, and we're all happy for you. We are also happy that the camera got back safe, and the film has been developed. Not only did you survive your ordeal, but you have made a tremendous difference by acquiring evidence that we can use to prove that time travel is possible. You are a hero, Mark. Your paycheck will be mailed to you by the end of this month. You certainly did enough to earn it, dear friend!"

He paused for a bit to pick up a notepad and take out a ballpoint pen. Peter then took a moment to adjust his glasses. He suddenly started looking a little tired.

"Now comes the part that's not so much fun."

"I have to answer a series of questions about precisely what happened?" I interrupted him.

"'Fraid so, Mark. It usually takes us about thirty minutes to an hour to get through this. Are you up for it now, or should we postpone this process to a later date?"

I thought about my decision. Part of me really did want to go home and collapse into my comfortable chair in front of my TV and watch a boring movie while I relaxed with a frozen meal. Yet another part of me wanted to get this last bit over with so that I wouldn't have to set a date to do it later. I opted for the second choice. Then something came to me in a flash. The camera! How could I let it slip my mind? Then I realized something else that made me wonder if one of the side effects of time travel was cognitive impairment. They just told me that the camera got back safe and the film was developed. How? We lost it, didn't we?

"The camera! We don't have it. We lost it," I told them. "But you just said the camera got back, and the pics were developed. I don't understand." I shook my head and knit my brows together, letting them know how perplexed I was.

I looked up and saw something I didn't expect. They all started grinning. What was going on here? I thought they would be upset.

Peter looked at me, grinned just slightly, and turned to his colleagues. They all looked like a bunch of people who were holding back a big surprise and wondering how I would react. I stared back at them, and then I remembered that the Finney could retrieve transported objects by themselves! Carrie couldn't find it because it had already gone back through time ahead of us.

"Interesting story there, Mark." Peter's response helped me to relax. It looked like he was about to tell me good news. "You may have lost it, but someone else found it. The camera was taken to a photography shop in the year 1900, and all the photographs were developed. They turned out well. The photographs and the camera have been preserved in historical archives ever since. For the past one hundred and nineteen years, people have been talking and sharing tales about the mysterious man and woman who posed with Jack Johnson and Isaac Cline. They also talked about how the man and woman interacted with the survivors during and after the storm. I looked at the pictures myself on the internet. I can only imagine how they will react when they see that both of you look exactly like the man and woman in that picture."

I looked at Peter and the rest. I then sighed a moment. I could hardly believe it. We did it. We accomplished our goal. Not only did we travel back in time, but we now had photographic evidence that we had done it. It was too good to be true. The proof had been preserved and waiting for us for one hundred nineteen years, though Carrie and I had gone through those years in a burst of light and a matter of moments. I leaned against the back of my chair and looked up at the ceiling. I felt like thanking God for our good fortune and the fact that everything had turned out good.

"Would you like to see the pictures, Mark?" Peter asked.

Did I ever. I nodded, and Peter reached into a briefcase next to his chair and pulled out a stack of brown-tinted black-and-white photographs. He spread them out on the desk. I looked at them. From the one on my far left to the one on my right and saw that they looked terrific. I saw Jack Johnson and Isaac Cline. I saw Carrie and me. I saw the pics of the aftermath of the storm. They looked amazing. I stared at them in a state of mesmerized awe.

"You ready to answer some questions now? By the way, we can have some copies of these made for you if you like. I know a good place in town where they can be framed. It's on us. Consider it our gift to you."

"Thanks," I answered. "I'll take you up on that. Um, yes, about questions, let's get them done. Ready when you are."

Peter shifted his weight in his chair and took a pen out of his shirt pocket and a stack of papers from a bag next to the desk. The printed forms appeared with questions and blanks on them to be filled out. The next several minutes consisted of Peter asking me questions about my time-travel journey. The questions could be divided into separate categories. At first, Peter asked me to describe the early and middle part of my journey and how I reacted to the stimuli of being in a new time and place. I answered to the best of my ability while straining to remember the details. Then Peter shifted to questions about how I reacted to the knowledge of the technical difficulties that occurred with the time machine. I admitted to them that I got nervous at that point, but I made an effort to stay calm. I then described how I assisted Carrie with helping others during the hurricane and managed to survive it.

I noticed that Carrie did not interrupt me at any point. I wondered if that was some sort of strict rule that supervisors like her had to obey: no interference with a new recruit when he or she was being debriefed. Eventually, after my long question-and-answer session was concluded, Peter closed his notepad and placed his pen back in his breast pocket.

"Well, that's it! We're done for today." He raised his eyebrows and looked around at all of us. "The mission was a success, and I will type up my official description of it tomorrow for our records. Good day, Mark, and I wish you a safe drive home. We will let you know later if we want to consider you for future missions, assuming that you're interested. Do you need someone to drive you, or do you think you can make it?"

I hesitated for a moment before responding. "I'm feeling pretty good now and definitely wide awake. I should be fine." I glanced at my wristwatch, which told me it was a few minutes past four in the afternoon on Saturday. I would be able to rest at home before resuming teaching duties at the college. Lucky me. I shook hands with Peter before leaving the room. I glanced back at Carrie, who was sitting comfortably with the others. She nodded at me as if she was letting me know without saying anything that I had done a good job. I appreciated her affirmation, and I wanted to say something to her in response. Somehow, I didn't think it was the right time. Not in front of the others. Maybe I could speak to her later.

She walked up to me. I looked at her and thought maybe I could bring it up now.

"Carrie?" I asked, feeling definitely awkward. Religion is always a touchy subject, and one I rarely touched.

"Yes," she replied.

"W-What if I wanted to become a Christian?"

She looked happy to hear my question. "Would you like to sit down?" She pointed toward a couple of chairs near the computers that were not being used. Most of the tech people had already gone home. We both sat.

"Do you really want to become a Christian by being born again?" Carrie asked.

"Yes," I answered quickly.

I was a bit surprised by how fast my reply was.

"I really don't know what born again means," I told her.

"A man named Nicodemus said the same thing," Carried said.

"Who?"

She started to answer, but I said, "Look. Something happened to me when we survived the storm and afterward. I saw something in you that I've never seen in anyone else. For a long time, I thought Christians were, at best, people believing in a set of fairy tales that gave them comfort and nothing else. You made me realize that I was wrong. Your faith is based on something beyond my ability to feel or comprehend. I can't put in words. I want that for myself. I spent my whole life thinking that the only thing that determined the difference between a good life and a wasted one was a matter of chance or sheer luck. I was wrong about that too."

I paused for a moment. I knew that I didn't want to ramble on too long. Carrie would no doubt want to get home soon.

"I felt something in the midst of the tragedy that made me realize that God must exist and really care about us. He's the one who gave you the ability to be strong while I kept struggling. You had a reassurance in the midst of the hurricane that I didn't have. It's not a placebo effect. I've studied placebo effects and always thought the effects of Christianity were a placebo, but faith in Christ is what made you strong, while I was weak."

Carrie looked down at her lap. I could see that she still had her Bible with her. How had I not noticed it? Then again, I was so distracted and rattled by my experience that it was easy for me to overlook things.

"Do you want to accept Christ as your Savior and say a prayer with me?" Carrie asked.

"Is that what I'm supposed to do?" I asked.

I nodded. I was so dazed by what was happening that it was difficult for me to speak just then.

Carrie led me through the prayer that I repeated after she gave me the words: "Lord, I know that I am a sinner. I have broken your laws. I accept you as my Lord and master. Come into my heart, and let me repent of all my sins. Amen."

Suddenly I had a feeling that was surprisingly similar to the feeling I had when Carrie and I got whisked back to our own time after the machine was activated. I felt like I was being lifted up, and I felt a sense of calm and peace unlike anything I'd ever experienced in my life. I knew that it didn't matter if I died today or tomorrow. I would go to the right place when I did. Just as she and I were extracted from the year 1900, I would be extracted from earth and taken to the right place eventually. I had no need to fear death.

I remember once when I was switching channels on my television set and heard a preacher giving a sermon. He said that for Christians, death was a shadow and not a reality. I chuckled at the time since the phrase sounded funny to me. This time I knew exactly what he meant. I knew it not just in my mind but in my heart.

Carrie smiled when I was done saying the prayer. "Would you like me to get you a Bible sometime?"

I grinned in response. "That would be nice, but don't think you have to pay for it. Just help me pick out a good translation."

"You bet. Well, I'm feeling a little tired. I think I'll go home. Keep in touch. Give me a call if you need anything."

I nodded and watched her walk away from me. For a lady who was tired, she was moving pretty good. I suddenly felt like I might need a wheelchair. Nevertheless, to my credit, I did manage to stumble through the tech room as I looked around and saw just a few people at their work spaces and dealing with the Finney. None of them turned to look at me. Strangely enough, I liked that. I suddenly had the intense desire to just get home without having to interact with anyone. I suddenly remembered how I felt when I interviewed for my teaching position so many years ago. I went home uncertain about the future and wondering what would happen. Now I wondered about my future in the time-travel project. Would they call me up again? Did I want to do it again? I wasn't exactly sure.

I left the building and got to my car and drove home. I was in a dazed state when I walked through the front door of my house. I looked around the living room and thought how unreal it all seemed to me now. I had been on a strange journey and now had to readjust to my normal time and place. I also had to adjust to being a whole new person because I now had a relationship with Jesus Christ. I sat down on the couch and looked at my smartphone. I needed to look for a Bible app for it. Which translation did I want? I wasn't sure. I knew from my history lessons that the King James Version was one of the oldest and had frequent use of words such as *thee, thou, thine*, and various other archaic English terms. Perhaps I could look for a more modern translation. What were they? I was stumped. I laughed to myself as I realized how clueless I was about my newfound faith. Like a freshman college student adjusting to their new academic environment, I now had to figure out so much.

I used my phone to go to my search engine to look up information on Bibles and came across one of the random articles that popped up there. It mentioned a man named John Newton. That name sounded familiar, and I couldn't help thinking that somehow it was relevant to my situation now. What was it that he did? I clicked on the article and found a brief bio on the man along with a poem that someone had recently written. The poem caught my attention, and I read it:

> A long time ago on a busy slave ship
> Lived a vain and wretched man
> He captured people and sold them abroad,
> All part of his greedy plan.
>
> He cared not for truth or the teachings of God.
> He thought they were all a lie.
> He mocked those who worshipped and earnestly
>     prayed
> Hoping their faith would die.
>
> Till one fateful night in a terrible storm
> The man feared that he might perish
> So he got on his knees and cried out to God,
> Expressing a simple wish:

"Lord, I know I am vile and destined for hell
For my life has been filled with sin.
A slave to my lusts I was all my years
And a blasphemer I have been.

But if you could just spare me from drowning
        this night,
I'll change my wicked ways
I'll study your word and be kinder to others
And I will occasionally pray."

So God spared the man, and he continued to live
Though his faith was often quite weak.
He returned to his sin and disobeyed God
And his future was again looking bleak.

Till finally the man allowed Christ in his heart
And made a swift change in careers.
He became a minister and preached throughout
England, God's truth to all who would hear.

Near the end of his life, the man began to go blind
But despite that he still loved the Lord,
For he knew that though God had let him go
        blind,
His spiritual sight He restored.

The man wrote many poems, sermons, and hymns,
One of them we still sing today.
Known throughout the world by millions of souls,
We call it Amazing Grace.

That's who John Newton was! He was the man who wrote the famous hymn. Suddenly I reflected on how I resembled the man described in that poem. Believing in a higher power but for so many years refusing to submit to him. This day I had. A weight had been lifted, and I felt his grace in a way that was impossible for me to ever experience before.

I relaxed on the couch and decided to see if I could find something on TV to watch. I put down my phone and turned on my television before switching to my Roku account. I looked at the stations and options provided. I decided to type in a movie in the search engine and see if it came up. It occurred to me that I might watch it then, since I obviously had nothing else to do. Sure enough, after typing in the title and clicking on search, the film appeared on screen for rental. It was one I hadn't seen in years.

I suddenly decided that I wasn't really interested in watching the movie. There was no way I could concentrate on it right now. Finding a Bible was far more important. I turned off the TV and resumed my search by typing in the words *Holy Bible* in the search engine to see what came up. I managed to find a Bible app that I downloaded and eventually clicked on so that I could read it. I would soon purchase a printed Bible as well, either at a bookstore or off the net. I opened my Bible app to one of the gospels and just started reading. It didn't take me long to get to a passage where it talked about Jesus being on a boat with his disciples. How appropriate for me. The passage described him walking on water and telling his disciples, "It is I; do not be afraid." I stopped reading and did a fast search that revealed that all four Gospels contain an account of Jesus in the midst of a sea with his disciples.

Suddenly I wondered if Carrie would want to hear from me later. She probably would. I would call her soon. Would she consider having me again as a coworker for another trip? One thing I knew for certain: we might be separated from each other in this world, but not for all eternity. I had made a choice that guaranteed that I would ultimately go to the same place she did, where all people exist outside the boundaries of time. I was looking forward to it. Jesus had calmed the storm for me, and I feared it no longer. He was calling me to him: *It is I. Do not be afraid.*

# Epilogue

I T WASN'T LONG AFTER THAT Carrie gave me a call to let me know that the team was willing to consider me for another trip, if I was interested. The archived photographs were shown to the general public as evidence that time travel is possible. A spokesperson for the time-travel project made an appearance on all the major news station shows in the area to describe what had been done. The reactions were, to put it mildly, somewhat mixed. Many believed while just as many claimed it was some sort of elaborate hoax. Others suggested that the tech people had simply created a very impressive and elaborate virtual reality experience so convincing that every subject involved believed it had really happened. This led to arguments and debates as to whether or not the people in charge of the whole thing had behaved in an ethical manner. Websites were started by believers and skeptics alike to report how people felt about the whole thing. Politicians, CNN news, and just about everybody in the media-dominated world was reacting one way or another. I wasn't asked to do any interviews personally because nobody knew I was involved except Carrie and the others on the team. I was told by them that I could certainly talk about it at this point since the cat had been let out of the bag, but somehow I didn't feel like it. I went back to teaching in the fall and waited for my next chance to have a time-traveling adventure. I eventually got a call from someone on the team telling me that they wanted to talk to me about that possibility, but that's another story.

# About the Author

MATTHEW RHOADS HAS BEEN WRITING stories since childhood. He's been fascinated with the subject of time travel for just as long. Matthew lives in central Arkansas with his wife, daughter, and two cats. *Turn Back Time* is his debut novel.